JANE B[…] 1917. In[…] composer […] to Europ[…] Mexico and Ceylon […] settling in Tangier in 1947.

She began to write *Two Serious Ladies*, a novel, when she was twenty-one. It was published in the United States in 1943 and, despite failing to achieve popular success, it gained an enormous 'underground' reputation. It was republished, in Britain, in 1965, followed by *Plain Pleasures*, a collection of stories, in 1966. Her play, *In the Summer House*, was first performed in 1951, and was produced on Broadway two years later.

In 1957 Jane Bowles suffered a stroke that left her unable to write. She died in Malaga in 1973.

This volume of Jane Bowles's stories consists of the collection *Plain Pleasures* and fictional pieces (Other Stories and From The Notebooks) that are fragments of larger, unfinished works, taken from Jane Bowles's notebooks dating from the 1940s and 1950s.

ARENA

Jane Bowles

PLAIN PLEASURES

and other stories

ARENA

An Arena Book

Published by Arrow Books Limited
17-21 Conway Street, London W1P 6JD

An imprint of the Hutchinson Publishing Group

London Melbourne Sydney Auckland
Johannesburg and agencies throughout
the world

First published in Great Britain by Peter Owen Ltd

This paperback edition 1985
Reprinted 1985

Printed and bound in Great Britain by
Anchor Brendon Limited, Tiptree, Essex

ISBN 0 09 935970 7

CONTENTS

PLAIN PLEASURES

Alva Perry was a dignified and reserved woman of Scotch and Spanish descent, in her early forties. She was still handsome, although her cheeks were too thin. Her eyes particularly were of an extraordinary clarity and beauty. She lived in her uncle's house, which had been converted into apartments, or tenements, as they were still called in her section of the country. The house stood on the side of a steep, wooded hill overlooking the main highway. A long cement staircase climbed halfway up the hill and stopped some distance below the house. It had originally led to a power station, which had since been destroyed. Mrs Perry had lived alone in her tenement since the death of her husband eleven years ago; however, she found small things to do all day long and she had somehow remained as industrious in her solitude as a woman who lives in the service of her family.

John Drake, an equally reserved person, occupied the tenement below hers. He owned a truck and engaged in free-lance work for lumber companies, as well as in the collection and delivery of milk cans for a dairy.

Mr Drake and Mrs Perry had never exchanged more than the simplest greeting in all the years that they had lived here in the hillside house.

One night Mr Drake, who was standing in the hall, heard Mrs Perry's heavy footsteps, which he had unconsciously learned to recognize. He looked up and saw her coming downstairs. She was dressed in a brown overcoat that had belonged to her dead husband, and she was hugging a paper bag to her bosom. Mr Drake offered to help her with the bag and she faltered, undecided, on the landing.

'They are only potatoes,' she said to him, 'but thank you very much. I am going to bake them out in the back yard. I have been meaning to for a long time.'

Mr Drake took the potatoes and walked with a stiff-jointed gait through the back door and down the hill to a short stretch of level land in back of the house which served as a yard. Here he put the paper bag on the ground. There was a big new incinerator smoking near the back stoop, and in the centre of the yard Mrs Perry's uncle had built a roofed-in pigpen faced in vivid artificial brick. Mrs Perry followed.

She thanked Mr Drake and began to gather twigs, scuttling rapidly between the edge of the woods and the pigpen, near which she was laying her fire. Mr Drake, without any further conversation, helped her to gather the twigs, so that when the fire was laid, she quite naturally invited him to wait and share the potatoes with her. He accepted and they sat in front of the fire on an overturned box.

Mr Drake kept his face averted from the fire and turned in the direction of the woods, hoping in this way to conceal somewhat his flaming-red cheeks from Mrs Perry. He was a very shy person and though his skin was naturally red all the time it turned to such deep crimson when he was in the presence of a strange woman that the change was distinctly noticeable. Mrs Perry wondered why he kept looking behind him, but she did not feel she knew him well enough to question him. She waited in vain for him to speak and then, realizing that he was not going to, she searched her own mind for something to say.

'Do you like plain ordinary pleasures?' she finally asked him gravely.

Mr Drake felt very much relieved that she had spoken and his colour subsided. 'You had better first give me a clearer notion of what you mean by ordinary pleasures, and then I'll tell you how I feel about them,' he answered soberly, halting after every few words, for he was as conscientious as he was shy.

Mrs Perry hesitated. 'Plain pleasures,' she began, 'like the ones that come without crowds or fancy food.' She searched her brain for more examples. 'Plain pleasures like this potato bake instead of dancing and whisky and bands. . . . Like a picnic but not the kind with a thousand extra things that get thrown out in a ditch because they don't get eaten up. I've seen grown people throw cakes away because they were too lazy to wrap them up and take them back home. Have you seen that go on?'

'No, I don't think so,' said Mr Drake.

'They waste a lot,' she remarked.

'Well, I do like plain pleasures,' put in Mr Drake, anxious that she should not lose the thread of the conversation.

'Don't you think that plain pleasures are closer to the heart of God?' she asked him.

He was a little embarrassed at her mentioning anything so solemn and so intimate on such short acquaintance, and he could not bring himself to answer her. Mrs Perry, who was ordinarily shut-mouthed, felt a stream of words swelling in her throat.

'My sister, Dorothy Alvarez,' she began without further introduction, 'goes to all gala affairs downtown. She has invited me to go and raise the dickens with her, but I won't go. She's the merriest one in her group and separated from her husband. They take her all the places with them. She can eat dinner in a restaurant every night if she wants to. She's crazy about fried fish and all kinds of things. I don't pay much mind to what I eat unless it's a potato bake like this. We each have only one single life which is our real life, starting at the cradle and ending at the grave. I warn Dorothy every time I see her that if she doesn't watch out her life is going to be left aching and starving on the side of the road and she's going to get to her grave without it. The farther a man follows the rainbow, the harder it is for him to get back to the life which he left starving like an old dog. Sometimes when a man gets older he has a revelation and wants awfully bad to get back to the place where he left his life, but he can't get to that place—not often. It's always better to stay alongside of your life. I told Dorothy that life was not a tree with a million different blossoms on it.' She reflected upon this for a moment in silence and then continued. 'She has a box that she puts pennies and nickels in when she thinks she's running around too much and she uses the money in the box to buy candles with for church. But that's all she'll do for her spirit, which is not enough for a grown woman.'

Mr Drake's face was strained because he was trying terribly hard to follow closely what she was saying, but he was so fearful lest she reveal some intimate secret of her sister's and later regret it that his mind was almost completely closed to everything else. He was fully prepared to stop her if she went too far.

The potatoes were done and Mrs Perry offered him two of them.

'Have some potatoes?' she said to him. The wind was colder now than when they had first sat down, and it blew around the pigpen.

'How do you feel about these cold howling nights that we have? Do you mind them?' Mrs Perry asked.

'I surely do,' said John Drake.

She looked intently at his face. 'He is as red as a cherry,' she said to herself.

'I might have preferred to live in a warm climate maybe.' Mr Drake was saying very slowly with a dreamy look in his eye, 'if I happened to believe in a lot of unnecessary changing around. A lot of going forth and back, I mean.' He blushed because he was approaching a subject that was close to his heart.

'Yes, yes, yes,' said Mrs Perry. 'A lot of switching around is no good.'

'When I was a younger man I had a chance to go way down south to Florida,' he continued. 'I had an offer to join forces with an alligator-farm project, but there was no security in the alligators. It might not have been a successful farm; it was not the risk that I minded so much, because I have always yearned to see palm trees and coconuts and the like. But I also believed that a man has to have a pretty good reason for moving around. I think that is what finally stopped me from going down to Florida and raising alligators. It was not the money, because I was not raised to give money first place. It was just that I felt then the way I do now, that if a man leaves home he must leave for some very good reason—like the boys who went to construct the Panama Canal or for any other decent reason. Otherwise I think he ought to stay in his own home town, so that nobody can say about him, "What does he think he can do here that we can't?" At least that is what I think people in a strange town would say about a man like myself if I landed there with some doubtful venture as my only excuse for leaving home. My brother don't feel that way. He never stays in one place more than three months.' He ate his potato with a woeful look in his eye, shaking his head from side to side.

Mrs Perry's mind was wandering, so that she was very much startled when he suddenly stood up and extended his hand to her.

'I'll leave now,' he said, 'but in return for the potatoes, will you come and have supper with me at a restaurant tomorrow night?'

She had not received an invitation of this kind in many years, having deliberately withdrawn from life in town, and she did not know how to answer him. 'Do you think I should do that?' she asked.

Mr Drake assured her that she should do it and she accepted his invitation.

On the following afternoon, Mrs Perry waited for the bus at the foot of the short cement bridge below the house. She needed help and advice from her sister about a lavender dress which no longer fitted her. She herself had never been able to sew well and she knew little about altering women's garments. She intended to wear her dress to the restaurant where she was to meet John Drake, and she was carrying it tucked under her arm.

Dorothy Alvarez lived on a side street in one half of a two-family house. She was seated in her parlour entertaining a man when Mrs Perry rang the bell. The parlour was immaculate but difficult to rest in because of the many bright and complicated patterns of the window curtains and the furniture covers, not the least disquieting of which was an enormous orange and black flowerpot design repeated a dozen times on the linoleum floor covering.

Dorothy pulled the curtain aside and peeked out to see who was ringing her bell. She was a curly-headed little person, with thick, unequal cheeks that were painted bright pink.

She was very much startled when she looked out and saw her sister, as she had not been expecting to see her until the following week.

'Oh!' Dorothy exclaimed.

'Who is it?' her guest asked.

'It's my sister. You better get out of here, because she must have something serious to talk to me about.

You better go out the back door. She don't like bumping up against strangers.'

The man was vexed, and left without bidding Dorothy good-bye. She ran to the door and let Mrs Perry in.

'Sit down,' she said, pulling her into the parlour. 'Sit down and tell me what's new.' She poured some hard candy from a paper bag into a glass dish.

'I wish you would alter this dress for me or help me do it,' said Mrs Perry. 'I want it for tonight. I'm meeting Mr Drake, my neighbour, at the restaurant down the street, so I thought I could dress in your house and leave from here. If you did the alteration yourself. I'd pay you for it.'

Dorothy's face fell. 'Why do you offer to pay me for it when I'm your sister?'

Mrs Perry looked at her in silence. She did not answer, because she did not know why herself. Dorothy tried the dress on her sister and pinned it here and there. 'I'm glad you're going out at last,' she said. 'Don't you want some beads?'

'I'll take some beads if you've got a spare string.'

'Well I hope this is the right guy for you,' said Dorothy, with her customary lack of tact. 'I would give anything for you to be in love, so you would quit living in that ugly house and come and live on some street nearby. Think how different everything would be for me. You'd be jollier too if you had a husband who was dear to you. Not like the last one. . . . I suppose I'll never stop dreaming and hoping,' she added nervously because she realized, but, as always, a little too late, that her sister hated to discuss such matters. 'Don't think,' she began weakly, 'that I'm so happy here all the time. I'm not so serious and solemn as you, of course. . . .'

'I don't know what you've been talking about,' said Alva Perry, twisting impatiently. 'I'm going out to have a dinner.'

'I wish you were closer to me,' whined Dorothy. 'I get blue in this parlour some nights.'

'I don't think you get very blue,' Mrs Perry remarked briefly.

'Well, as long as you're going out, why don't you pep up?'

'I am pepped up,' replied Mrs Perry.

Mrs Perry closed the restaurant door behind her and walked the full length of the room, peering into each booth in search of her escort. He had apparently not yet arrived, so she chose an empty booth and seated herself inside on the wooden bench. After fifteen minutes she decided that he was not coming and, repressing the deep hurt that this caused her, she focused her full attention on the menu and succeeded in shutting Mr Drake from her mind. While she was reading the menu, she unhooked her string of beads and tucked them away in her purse. She had called the waitress and was ordering pork when Mr Drake arrived. He greeted her with a timid smile.

'I see that you are ordering your dinner,' he said, squeezing into his side of the booth. He looked with admiration at her lavender dress, which exposed her pale chest. He would have preferred that she be bare-headed because he loved women's hair. She had on an ungainly black felt hat which she always wore in every kind of weather. Mr Drake remembered with intense pleasure the potato bake in front of the fire and he was much more excited than he had imagined he would be to see her once again.

Unfortunately she did not seem to have any impulse to communicate with him and his own tongue was silenced in a very short time. They ate the first half of their meal without saying anything at all to each other. Mr Drake had ordered a bottle of sweet wine and after Mrs Perry had finished her second glass she finally spoke. 'I think they cheat you in restaurants.'

He was pleased she had made any remark at all, even though it was of an ungracious nature.

'Well, it is usually to be among the crowd that we pay large prices for small portions,' he said, much to his own surprise, for he had always considered himself a lone wolf, and his behaviour had never belied this. He sensed this same quality in Mrs Perry, but he was moved by a strange desire to mingle with her among the flock.

'Well, don't you think what I say is true?' he asked

hesitantly. There appeared on his face a curious, dislocated smile and he held his head in an outlandishly erect position which betrayed his state of tension.

Mrs Perry wiped her plate clean with a piece of bread. Since she was not in the habit of drinking more than once every few years, the wine was going very quickly to her head.

'What time does the bus go by the door here?' she asked in a voice that was getting remarkably loud.

'I can find out for you if you really want to know. Is there any reason why you want to know now?'

'I've got to get home some time so I can get up tomorrow morning.'

'Well, naturally I will take you home in my truck when you want to go, but I hope you won't go yet.' He leaned forward and studied her face anxiously.

'I can get home all right,' she answered him glumly, 'and it's just as good now as later.'

'Well, no, it isn't,' he said, deeply touched, because there was no longer any mistaking her distinctly inimical attitude. He felt that he must at any cost keep her with him and enlist her sympathies. The wine was contributing to this sudden aggressiveness, for it was not usually in his nature to make any effort to try to get what he wanted. He now began speaking to her earnestly and quickly.

'I want to share a full evening's entertainment with you, or even a week of entertainment,' he said, twisting nervously on his bench. 'I know where all the roadside restaurants and dance houses are situated all through the county. I am master of my truck, and no one can stop me from taking a vacation if I want to. It's a long time since I took a vacation—not since I was handed out my yearly summer vacation when I went to school. I never spent any real time in any of these roadside houses, but I know the proprietors, nearly all of them, because I have lived here all of my life. There is one dance hall that is built on a lake. I know the proprietor. If we went there, we could stray off and walk around the water, if that was agreeable to you.' His face was a brighter red than ever and he appeared to be temporarily stripped of the reserved and cautious demeanour that had so characterized him the evening before. Some quality in Mrs Perry's nature which he had only dimly perceived at first now sounded like a deep bell within himself because of her anger and he was flung backward into a forgotten and weaker state of being. His yearning for a word of kindness from her increased every minute.

Mrs Perry sat drinking her wine more and more quickly and her resentment mounted with each new glass.

'I know all the proprietors of dance houses in the county also,' she said. 'My sister Dorothy Alvarez has them up to her house for beer when they take a holiday. I've got no need to meet anybody new or see any new places. I even know this place we are eating in from a long time ago. I had dinner here with my husband a few times.' She looked around her. 'I remember *him*,' she said, pointing a long arm at the proprietor, who had just stepped out of the kitchen.

'How are you after these many years?' she called to him.

Mr Drake was hesitant about what to do. He had not realized that Mrs Perry was getting as drunk as she seemed to be now. Ordinarily he would have felt embarrassed and would have hastened to lead her out of the restaurant, but he thought that she might be more approachable drunk and nothing else mattered to him. 'I'll stay with you for as long as you like,' he said.

His words spun around in Mrs Perry's mind. 'What are you making a bid for, anyway?' she asked him, leaning back heavily against the bench.

'Nothing dishonourable,' he said. 'On the contrary, something extremely honourable if you will accept.' Mr Drake was so distraught that he did not know exactly what he was saying, but Mrs Perry took his words to mean a proposal of marriage, which was unconsciously what he had hoped she would do. Mrs Perry looked at even this exciting offer through the smoke of her resentment.

'I suppose,' she said smiling joylessly, 'that you would like a lady to mash your potatoes for you three times a day. But I am not a mashed-potato masher and I never have been. I would prefer,' she added, raising her voice, 'I would prefer to have *him* mash my potatoes for *me* in a big restaurant kitchen.' She nodded in the direction of the proprietor, who had remained standing in front of the kitchen door so that he could watch Mrs Perry. This time he grinned and winked his eye.

Mrs Perry fumbled through the contents of her purse in search of a handkerchief and, coming upon her sister's string of beads, she pulled them out and laid them in her gravy. 'I am not a mashed-potato masher,' she repeated, and then without warning she clambered out of the booth and lumbered down the aisle. She disappeared up a dark brown staircase at the back of the restaurant. Both Mr Drake and the proprietor assumed that she was going to the ladies' toilet.

Actually Mrs Perry was not specifically in search of the toilet, but rather for any place where she could be alone. She walked down the hall upstairs and jerked open a door on her left, closing it behind her. She stood in total darkness for a minute, and then, feeling a chain brush her forehead, she yanked at it brutally, lighting the room from a naked ceiling bulb, which she almost pulled down together with its fixtures.

She was standing at the foot of a double bed with a high Victorian headboard. She looked around her and, noticing a chair placed underneath a small window, she walked over to it and pushed the window open, securing it with a short stick; then she sat down.

'This is perfection,' she said aloud, glaring at the ugly little room. 'This is surely a gift from the Lord.'

She squeezed her hands together until her knuckles were white. 'Oh, how I love it here! How I love it! How I love it!'

She flung one arm out over the window sill in a gesture of abandon, but she had not noticed that the rain was teeming down, and it soaked her lavender sleeve in a very short time.

'Mercy me!' she remarked, grinning. 'It's raining here. The people at the dinner tables don't get the rain, but I do and I like it!' She smiled benignly at the rain. She sat there half awake and half asleep and then slowly she felt a growing certainty that she could reach her own room from where she was sitting without ever returning to the restaurant. 'I have kept the pathway open all my life,' she muttered in a thick voice, 'so that I could get back.'

A few moments later she said, 'I am sitting there.' An expression of malevolent triumph transformed her face and she made a slight effort to stiffen her back. She remained for a long while in the stronghold of this fantasy, but it gradually faded and in the end dissolved. When she drew her cold shaking arm in out of the rain, the tears were streaming down her cheeks. Without ceasing to cry she crept on to the big double bed and fell asleep, face downward with her hat on.

Meanwhile the proprietor had come quietly upstairs, hoping that he would bump into her as she came out of the ladies' toilet. He had been flattered by her attention and he judged that in her present drunken state it would be easy to sneak a kiss from her and perhaps even more. When he saw the beam of light shining under his own bedroom door, he stuck his tongue out over his lower lip and smiled. Then he tiptoed down the stairs, plotting on the way what he would tell Mr Drake.

Everyone had left the restaurant, and Mr Drake was walking up and down the aisle when the proprietor reached the bottom of the staircase.

'I am worried about my lady friend,' Mr Drake said, hurrying up to him. 'I am afraid that she may have passed out in the toilet.'

'The truth is,' the proprietor answered, 'that she has passed out in an empty bedroom upstairs. Don't worry about it. My daughter will take care of her if she wakes up feeling sick. I used to know her husband. You can't do nothing about her now.' He put his hands into his pockets and looked solemnly into Mr Drake's eyes.

Mr Drake, not being equal to such a delicate situation, paid his bill and left. Outside he crawled into his freshly painted red truck and sat listening desolately to the rain.

The next morning Mrs Perry awakened a little after sunrise. Thanks to her excellent constitution she did not feel very sick, but she lay motionless on the bed looking around her at the walls for a long time. Slowly she remembered that this room she was lying in was above the restaurant, but she did not know how she had gotten there. She remembered the dinner with Mr Drake, but not much of what she had said to him. It did not occur to her to blame him for her present circumstance. She was not hysterical at finding herself in a strange bed because, although she was a very tense and nervous woman, she possessed great depth of emotion and only certain things concerned her personally.

She felt very happy and she thought of her uncle who had passed out at a convention fifteen years ago. He had walked around the town all the morning without knowing where he was. She smiled.

After resting a little while longer, she got out of bed and clothed herself. She went into the hall and found the staircase and she descended with bated breath and a fast-beating heart, because she was so eager to get back down into the restaurant.

It was flooded with sunshine and still smelled of meat and sauce. She walked a little unsteadily down the aisle between the rows of wooden booths and tables. The tables were all bare and scrubbed clean. She looked anxiously from one to the other, hoping to select the booth they had sat in, but she was unable to choose among them. The tables were all identical. In a moment this anonymity served only to heighten her tenderness.

'John Drake,' she whispered. 'My sweet John Drake.'

EVERYTHING IS NICE

The highest street in the blue Moslem town skirted the edge of a cliff. She walked over to the thick protecting wall and looked down. The tide was out, and the flat dirty rocks below were swarming with skinny boys. A Moslem woman came up to the blue wall and stood next to her, grazing her hip with the basket she was carrying. She pretended not to notice her, and kept her eyes fixed on a white dog that had just slipped down the side of a rock and plunged into a crater of sea-water. The sound of its bark was earsplitting. Then the woman jabbed the basket firmly into her ribs, and she looked up.

'That one is a porcupine,' said the woman, pointing a henna-stained finger into the basket.

This was true. A large dead porcupine lay there, with a pair of new yellow socks folded on top of it.

She looked again at the woman. She was dressed in a *haik*, and the white cloth covering the lower half of her face was loose, about to fall down.

'I am Zodelia,' she announced in a high voice. 'And you are Betsoul's friend.' The loose cloth slipped below her chin and hung there like a bib. She did not pull it up.

'You sit in her house and you sleep in her house and you eat in her house,' the woman went on, and she nodded in agreement. 'Your name is Jeanie and you live in a hotel with other Nazarenes. How much does the hotel cost you?'

A loaf of bread shaped like a disc flopped on to the ground from inside the folds of the woman's *haik*, and she did not have to answer her question. With some difficulty the woman picked the loaf up and stuffed it in between the quills of the porcupine and the basket handle. Then she set the basket down on the top of the blue wall and turned to her with bright eyes.

'I am the people in the hotel,' she said. 'Watch me.'

She was pleased because she knew that the woman who called herself Zodelia was about to present her with a little skit. It would be delightful to watch, since all the people of the town spoke and gesticulated as though they had studied at the *Comédie Française*.

'The people in the hotel,' Zodelia announced,

formally beginning her skit. 'I am the people in the hotel.'

' "Good-bye, Jeanie, good-bye. Where are you going?"

' "I am going to a Moslem house to visit my Moslem friends, Betsoul and her family. I will sit in a Moslem room and eat Moslem food and sleep on a Moslem bed."

' "Jeanie, Jeanie, when will you come back to us in the hotel and sleep in your own room?"

' "I will come back to you in three days. I will come back and sit in a Nazarene room and eat Nazarene food and sleep on a Nazarene bed. I will spend half the week with Moslem friends and half with Nazarenes." '

The woman's voice had a triumphant ring as she finished her sentence; then, without announcing the end of the sketch, she walked over to the wall and put one arm around her basket.

Down below, just at the edge of the cliff's shadow, a Moslem woman was seated on a rock, washing her legs in one of the holes filled with sea-water. Her *haik* was piled on her lap and she was huddled over it, examining her feet.

'She is looking at the ocean,' said Zodelia.

She was not looking at the ocean; with her head down and the mass of cloth in her lap she could not possibly have seen it; she would have had to straighten up and turn around.

'She is *not* looking at the ocean,' she said.

'She is looking at the ocean,' Zodelia repeated, as if she had not spoken.

She decided to change the subject. 'Why do you have a porcupine with you?' she asked her, although she knew that some of the Moslems, particularly the country people, enjoyed eating them.

'It is a present for my aunt. Do you like it?'

'Yes,' she said. 'I like porcupines. I like big porcupines and little ones, too.'

Zodelia seemed bewildered, and then bored, and she decided she had somehow ruined the conversation by mentioning small porcupines.

'Where is your mother?' Zodelia said at length.

'My mother is in her country in her own house,' she said automatically; she had answered the question a hundred times.

'Why don't you write her a letter and tell her to come here? You can take her on a promenade and show her the ocean. After that she can go back to her own country and sit in her house.' She picked up her basket and adjusted the strip of cloth over her mouth. 'Would you like to go to a wedding?' she asked her.

She said she would love to go to a wedding, and they started off down the crooked blue street, heading into the wind. As they passed a small shop Zodelia stopped. 'Stand here,' she said. 'I want to buy something.'

After studying the display for a minute or two Zodelia poked her and pointed to some cakes inside a square box with glass sides. 'Nice?' she asked her. 'Or not nice?'

The cakes were dusty and coated with a thin, ugly-coloured icing. They were called *Galletas Ortiz*.

'They are very nice,' she replied, and bought her a dozen of them. Zodelia thanked her briefly and they walked on. Presently they turned off the street into a narrow alley and started downhill. Soon Zodelia stopped at a door on the right, and lifted the heavy brass knocker in the form of a fist.

'The wedding is here?' she said to her.

Zodelia shook her head and looked grave. 'There is no wedding here,' she said.

A child opened the door and quickly hid behind it, covering her face. She followed Zodelia across the black and white tile floor of the closed *patio*. The walls were washed in blue, and a cold light shone through the broken panes of glass far above their heads. There was a door on each side of the *patio*. Outside one of them, barring the threshold, was a row of pointed slippers. Zodelia stepped out of her own shoes and set them down near the others.

She stood behind Zodelia and began to take off her own shoes. It took her a long time because there was a knot in one of her laces. When she was ready, Zodelia took her hand and pulled her along with her into a dimly lit room, where she led her over to a mattress which lay against the wall.

'Sit,' she told her, and she obeyed. Then without further comment she walked off, heading for the far end of the room. Because her eyes had not grown used to the dimness, she had the impression of a figure disappearing down a long corridor. Then she began to see the brass bars of a bed, glowing weakly in the darkness.

Only a few feet away, in the middle of the carpet, sat an old lady in a dress made of green and purple curtain fabric. Through the many rents in the material she could see the printed cotton dress and the tan sweater underneath. Across the room several women sat along another mattress, and further along the mattress three babies were sleeping in a row, each one close against the wall with its head resting on a fancy cushion.

'Is it nice here?' It was Zodelia, who had returned without her *haik*. Her black crêpe European dress hung unbelted down to her ankles, almost grazing her bare feet. The hem was lopsided. 'Is it nice here?' she asked again, crouching on her haunches in front of her and pointing at the old woman. 'That one is Tetum,' she said. The old lady plunged both hands into a bowl of raw chopped meat and began shaping the stuff into little balls.

'Tetum' echoed the ladies on the mattress.

'This Nazarene,' said Zodelia, gesturing in her

direction, 'spends half her time in a Moslem house with Moslem friends and the other half in a Nazarene hotel with other Nazarenes.'

'That's nice,' said the women opposite. 'Half with Moslem friends and half with Nazarenes.'

The old lady looked very stern. She noticed that her bony cheeks were tattoed with tiny blue crosses.

'Why?' asked the old lady abruptly in a deep voice. '*Why* does she spend half her time with Moslem friends and half with Nazarenes?' She fixed her eye on Zodelia, never ceasing to shape the meat with her swift fingers. Now she saw that her knuckles were also tattooed with blue crosses.

Zodelia stared back at her stupidly. 'I don't know why,' she said, shrugging one fat shoulder. It was clear that the picture she had been painting for them had suddenly lost all its charm for her.

'Is she crazy?' the old lady asked.

'No,' Zodelia answered listlessly. 'She is not crazy.' There were shrieks of laughter from the mattress.

The old lady fastened her sharp eyes on the visitor, and she saw that they were heavily outlined in black. 'Where is your husband?' she demanded.

'He's travelling in the desert.'

'Selling things,' Zodelia put in. This was the popular explanation for her husband's trips; she did not try to contradict it.

'Where is your mother?' the old lady asked.

'My mother is in our country in her own house.'

'Why don't you go and sit with your mother in her own house?' she scolded. 'The hotel costs a lot of money.'

'In the city where I was born,' she began, 'there are many, many automobiles and many, many trucks.'

The women on the mattress were smiling pleasantly. 'Is that true?' remarked the one in the centre in a tone of polite interest.

'I hate trucks,' she told the woman with feeling.

The old lady lifted the bowl of meat off her lap and set it down on the carpet. 'Trucks are nice,' she said severely.

'That's true,' the women agreed, after only a moment's hesitation. 'Trucks are very nice.'

'Do *you* like trucks?' she asked Zodelia, thinking that because of their relatively greater intimacy she might perhaps agree with her.

'Yes,' she said. 'They are nice. Trucks are very nice.' She seemed lost in meditation, but only for an instant. 'Everything is nice,' she announced with a look of triumph.

'It's the truth,' the women said from their mattress. 'Everything is nice.'

They all looked happy, but the old lady was still frowning. 'Aicha!' she yelled, twisting her neck so that her voice could be heard in the *patio*. 'Bring the tea!'

Several little girls came into the room carrying the tea things and a low round table.

'Pass the cakes to the Nazarene,' she told the smallest child, who was carrying a cut-glass dish piled with cakes. She saw that they were the ones she had bought for Zodelia; she did not want any of them. She wanted to go home.

'Eat!' the women called out from their mattress. 'Eat the cakes.'

The child pushed the glass dish forward.

'The dinner at the hotel is ready,' she said, standing up.

'Drink tea,' said the old woman scornfully. 'Later you will sit with the other Nazarenes and eat their food.'

'The Nazarenes will be angry if I'm late.' She realized that she was lying stupidly, but she could not stop. 'They will hit me!' She tried to look wild and frightened.

'Drink tea. They will not hit you,' the old woman told her. 'Sit down and drink tea.'

The child was still offering her the glass dish as she backed away toward the door. Outside she sat down on the black and white tiles to lace her shoes. Only Zodelia followed her into the *patio*.

'Come back,' the others were calling. 'Come back into the room.'

Then she noticed the porcupine basket standing nearby against the wall. 'Is that old lady in the room your aunt? Is she the one you were bringing the porcupine to?' she asked her.

'No. She is not my aunt.'

'Where *is* your aunt?'

'My aunt is in her own house.'

'When will you take the porcupine to her?' She wanted to keep talking, so that Zodelia would be distracted and forget to fuss about her departure.

'The porcupine sits here,' she said firmly. 'In my own house.'

She decided not to ask her again about the wedding. When they reached the door Zodelia opened it just enough to let her through. 'Good-bye,' she said behind her. 'I shall see you tomorrow, if Allah wills it.'

'When?'

'Four o'clock.' It was obvious that she had chosen the first figure that had come into her head. Before closing the door she reached out and pressed two of the dry Spanish cakes into her hand. 'Eat them,' she said graciously. 'Eat them at the hotel with the other Nazarenes.'

She started up the steep alley, headed once again for the walk along the cliff. The houses on either side of her were so close that she could smell the dampness of the walls and feel it on her cheeks like a thicker air.

When she reached the place where she had met Zodelia she went over to the wall and leaned on it. Although the sun had sunk behind the houses, the sky was still luminous and the blue of the wall had deepened. She rubbed her fingers along it: the wash was fresh and a little of the powdery stuff came off. And she remembered how once she had reached out to touch the face of a clown because it had awakened some longing. It had happened at a little circus, but not when she was a child.

A GUATEMALAN IDYLL

When the traveller arrived at the pension the wind was blowing hard. Before going in to have the hot soup he had been thinking about, he left his luggage inside the door and walked a few blocks in order to get an idea of the town. He came to a very large arch through which, in the distance, he could see a plain. He thought he could distinguish figures seated around a far-away fire, but he was not certain because the wind made tears in his eyes.

'How dismal,' he thought, letting his mouth drop open. 'But never mind. Brace up. It's probably a group of boys and girls sitting around an open fire having a fine time together. The world is the world, after all is said and done, and a patch of grass in one place is green the way it is in any other.'

He turned back and walked along quickly, skirting the walls of the low stone houses. He was a little worried that he might not be able to recognize the door of his pension.

'There's not supposed to be any variety in the U.S.A.,' he said to himself. 'But this Spanish architecture beats everything, it's so monotonous.' He knocked on one of the doors, and shortly a child with a shaved head appeared. With a strong American accent he said to her: 'Is this the Pension Espinoza?'

'*Sí!*' The child led him inside to a fountain in the centre of a square *patio*. He looked into the basin and the child did too.

'There are four fish inside here,' she said to him in Spanish. 'Would you like me to try and catch one of them for you?'

The traveller did not understand her. He stood there uncomfortably, longing to go to his room. The little girl was still trying to get hold of a fish when her mother, who owned the pension, came out and joined them. The woman was quite fat, but her face was small and pointed, and she wore glasses attached by a gold chain to her dress. She shook hands with him and asked him in fairly good English if he had had a pleasant journey.

'He wants to see some of the fish,' explained the child.

'Certainly,' said Señora Espinoza, moving her hands about in the water with dexterity. 'Soon now, soon now,' she said, laughing as one of the fish slipped between her fingers.

The traveller nodded. 'I would like to go to my room,' he said.

The American was a little dismayed by his room. There were four brass beds in a row, all of them very old and a little crooked.

'God!' he said to himself. 'They'll have to remove some of these beds. They give me the willies.'

A cord hung down from the ceiling. On the end of it at the height of his nose was a tiny electric bulb. He turned it on and looked at his hands under the light. They were chapped and dirty. A barefoot servant girl came in with a pitcher and a bowl.

In the dining-room calendars decorated the walls, and there was an elaborate cut-glass carafe on every table. Several people had already begun their meal in silence. One little girl was speaking in a high voice.

'I'm not going to the band concert tonight, Mamá,' she was saying.

'Why not?' asked her mother with her mouth full. She looked seriously at her daughter.

'Because I don't like to hear music. I hate it!'

'Why?' asked her mother absently, taking another large mouthful of her food. She spoke in a deep voice like a man's. Her head, which was set low between her shoulders, was covered with black curls. Her chin was heavy and her skin was dark and coarse; however, she had very beautiful blue eyes. She sat with her legs apart, with one arm lying flat on the table. The child bore no resemblance to her mother. She was frail, with stiff hair of the peculiar light colour that is often found in mulattos. Her eyes were so pale that they seemed almost white.

As the traveller came in, the child turned to look at him.

'Now there are nine people eating in this pension,' she said immediately.

'Nine,' said her mother. 'Many mouths.' She pushed her plate aside wearily and looked up at the calendar beside her on the wall. At last she turned around and saw the stranger. Having already finished her own dinner, she followed the progress of his meal with interest. Once she caught his eye.

'Good appetite,' she said, nodding gravely, and then she watched his soup until he had finished it.

'My pills,' she said to Lilina, holding her hand out without turning her head. To amuse herself, Lilina emptied the whole bottle into her mother's hand.

'Now you have your pills,' she said. When Señora Ramirez realized what had happened, she dealt Lilina a terrible blow in the face, using the hand which held the pills, and thus leaving them sticking to the child's moist skin and in her hair. The traveller turned. He was so bored and at the same time disgusted by what he saw that he decided he had better look for another pension that very night.

'Soon,' said the waitress, putting his meat in front of him, 'the musician will come. For fifty cents he will play you all the songs you want to hear. One night would not be time enough. *She* will be out of the room by then.' She looked over at Lilina, who was squealing like a stuck pig.

'Those pills cost me three *quetzales* a bottle,' Señora Ramirez complained. One of the young men at a nearby table came over and examined the empty bottle. He shook his head.

'A barbarous thing,' he said.

'What a dreadful child you are, Lilina!' said an English lady, who was seated at quite a distance from everybody else. All the diners looked up. Her face and neck were quite red with annoyance. She was speaking to them in English.

'Can't you behave like civilized people?' she demanded.

'You be quiet, you!' The young man had finished examining the empty pill bottle. His companions burst out laughing.

'O.K., girl,' he continued in English. 'Want a piece of chewing gum?' His companions were quite helpless with laughter at his last remark, and all three of them got up and left the room. Their guffaws could be heard from the *patio* where they had grouped around the fountain, fairly doubled up.

'It's a disgrace to the adult mind,' said the English lady. Lilina's nose had started to bleed, and she rushed out.

'And tell Consuelo to hurry in and eat her dinner,' her mother called after her. Just then the musician arrived. He was a small man and he wore a black suit and a dirty shirt.

'Well,' said Lilina's mother. 'At last you came.'

'I was having dinner with my uncle. Time passes, Señora Ramirez! *Gracias a Dios!*'

'*Gracias a Dios* nothing! It's unheard-of having to eat dinner without music.'

The violinist fell into a chair, and, bent over low, he started to play with all his strength.

'Waltzes!' shouted Señora Ramirez above the music. 'Waltzes!' She looked petulant and at the same time as though she were about to cry. As a matter of fact, the stranger was quite sure that he saw a tear roll down her cheek.

'Are you going to the band concert tonight?' she asked him; she spoke English rather well.

'I don't know. Are you?'

'Yes, with my daughter Consuelo. If the unfortunate girl ever gets here to eat her supper. She doesn't like food. Only dancing. She dances like a real butterfly. She has French blood from me. She is of a much better type than the little one, Lilina, who is always hurting; hurting me, hurting her sister, hurting her friends. I hope that God will have pity on her.' At this she really did shed a tear or two, which she brushed away with her napkin.

'Well, she's young yet,' said the stranger. Señora Ramirez agreed heartily.

'Yes, she is young.' She smiled at him sweetly and seemed quite content.

Lilina meanwhile was in her room, standing over the white bowl in which they washed their hands, letting the blood drip into it. She was breathing heavily like someone who is trying to simulate anger.

'Stop that breathing! You sound like an old man,' said her sister Consuelo, who was lying on the bed with a hot brick on her stomach. Consuelo was small and dark, with a broad flat face and an unusually narrow skull. She had a surly nature, which is often the case when young girls do little else but dream of a lover. Lilina, who was a bully without any curiosity concerning the grown-up world, hated her sister more than anyone else she knew.

'Mamá says that if you don't come in to eat soon she will hit you.'

'Is that how *you* got that bloody nose?'

'No,' said Lilina. She walked away from the basin and her eye fell on her mother's corset which was lying on the bed. Quickly she picked it up and went with it into the *patio*, where she threw it into the fountain. Consuelo, frightened by the appropriation of the corset, got up hastily and arranged her hair.

'Too much upset for a girl of my age,' she said to

herself, patting her stomach. Crossing the *patio* she saw Señorita Córdoba walking along, holding her head very high as she slipped some hairpins more firmly into the bun at the back of her neck. Consuelo felt like a frog or a beetle walking behind her. Together they entered the dining-room.

'Why don't you wait for midnight to strike?' said Señora Ramirez to Consuelo. Señorita Córdoba, assuming that this taunt had been addressed to her, bridled and stiffened. Her eyes narrowed and she stood still. Señora Ramirez, a gross coward, gave her a strange idiotic smile.

'How is your health, Señorita Córdoba?' she asked softly, and then feeling confused, she pointed to the stranger and asked him if he knew Señorita Córdoba.

'No, no; he does not know me.' She held out her hand stiffly to the stranger and he took it. No names were mentioned.

Consuelo sat down beside her mother and ate voraciously, a sad look in her eye. Señorita Córdoba ordered only fruit. She sat looking out into the dark *patio*, giving the other diners a view of the nape of her neck. Presently she opened a letter and began to read. The others all watched her closely. The three young men who had laughed so heartily before were now smiling like idiots, waiting for another such occasion to present itself.

The musician was playing a waltz at the request of Señora Ramirez, who was trying her best to attract again the attention of the stranger. 'Tra-la-la-la,' she sang, and in order better to convey the beauty of the waltz she folded her arms in front of her and rocked from side to side.

'Ay, Consuelo! It is for her to waltz,' she said to the stranger. 'There will be many people in the *plaza* tonight, and there is so much wind. I think that you must fetch my shawl, Consuelo. It is getting very cold.'

While awaiting Consuelo's return she shivered and picked her teeth.

The traveller thought she was crazy and a little disgusting. He had come here as a buyer for a very important textile concern. Having completed all his work, he had for some reason decided to stay on another week, perhaps because he had always heard that a vacation in a foreign country was a desirable thing. Already he regretted his decision, but there was no boat out before the following Monday. By the end of the meal he was in such despair that his face wore a peculiarly young and sensitive look. In order to buoy himself up a bit, he began to think about what he would get to eat three weeks hence, seated at his mother's table on Thanksgiving Day. They would be very glad to hear that he had not enjoyed himself on this trip because they had always considered it something in the nature of a betrayal when anyone in the family expressed a desire to travel. He thought they led a fine life and was inclined to agree with them.

Consuelo had returned with her mother's shawl. She

was dreaming again when her mother pinched her arm.

'Well, Consuelo, are you coming to the band concert or are you going to sit here like a dummy? I daresay the Señor is not coming with us, but *we* like music, so get up, and we will say good-night to this gentleman and be on our way.'

The traveller had not understood this speech. He was therefore very much surprised when Señora Ramirez tapped him on the shoulder and said to him severely in English: 'Good night, Señor. Consuelo and I are going to the band concert. We will see you tomorrow at breakfast.'

'Oh, but I'm going to the band concert myself,' he said, in a panic least they leave him with a whole evening on his hands.

Señora Ramirez flushed with pleasure. The three walked down the badly lit street together, escorted by a group of skinny yellow dogs.

'These old grilled windows are certainly very beautiful,' the traveller said to Señora Ramirez. 'Old as the hills themselves, aren't they?'

'You must go to the capital if you want beautiful buildings,' said Señora Ramirez. 'Very new and clean they are.'

'I should think,' he said, 'that these old buildings were your point of interest here, aside from your Indians and their native costumes.'

They walked on for a little while in silence. A small

boy came up to them and tried to sell them some lollipops.

'Five *centavos*,' said the little boy.

'Absolutely not,' said the traveller. He had been warned that the natives would cheat him, and he was actually enraged every time they approached him with their wares.

'Four *centavcs* . . . three *centavos*. . . .'

'No, no, no! Go away!' The little boy ran ahead of them.

'I would like a lollipop,' said Consuelo to him.

'Well, why didn't you say so, then?' he demanded.

'No,' said Consuelo.

'She does not mean no,' explained her mother. 'She can't learn to speak English. She has clouds in her head.'

'I see,' said the traveller. Consuelo looked mortified. When they came to the end of the street, Señora Ramirez stood still and lowered her head like a bull.

'Listen,' she said to Consuelo. 'Listen. You can hear the music from here.'

'Yes, Mamá. Indeed you can.' They stood listening to the faint *marimba* noise that reached them. The traveller sighed.

'Please, let's get going if we *are* going,' he said. 'Otherwise there is no point.'

The square was already crowded when they arrived. The older people sat on benches under the trees, while the younger ones walked round and round, the girls in one direction and the boys in the other. The musicians played inside a kiosk in the centre of the square. Señora Ramirez led both Consuelo and the stranger into the girls' line, and they had not been walking more than a minute before she settled into a comfortable gait, with an expression very much like that of someone relaxing in an armchair.

'We have three hours,' she said to Consuelo.

The stranger looked around him. Many of the girls were barefoot and pure Indian. They walked along holding tightly to one another, and were frequently convulsed with laughter.

The musicians were playing a formless but militant-sounding piece which came to many climaxes without ending. The drummer was the man who had just played the violin at Señora Espinoza's pension.

'Look!' said the traveller excitedly. 'Isn't that the man who was just playing for us at dinner. He must have run all the way. I'll bet he's sweating some.'

'Yes, it is he,' said Señora Ramirez. 'The nasty little rat. I would like to tear him right off his stand. Remember the one at the Grand Hotel, Consuelo? He stopped at every table, Señor, and I have never seen such beautiful teeth in my life. A smile on his face from the moment he came into the room until he went out again. This one looks at his shoes while he is playing, and he would like to kill us all.'

Some big boys threw confetti into the traveller's face.

'I wonder,' he asked himself. 'I wonder what kind of

fun they get out of just walking around and around this little park and throwing confetti at each other.'

The boys' line was in a constant uproar about something. The broader their smiles became, the more he suspected them of plotting something, probably against him, for apparently he was the only tourist there that evening. Finally he was so upset that he walked along looking up at the stars, or even for short stretches with his eyes shut, because it seemed to him that somehow this rendered him a little less visible. Suddenly he caught sight of Señorita Córdoba. She was across the street buying lollipops from a boy.

'Señorita!' He waved his hand from where he was, and then joyfully bounded out of the line and across the street. He stood panting by her side, while she reddened considerably and did not know what to say to him.

Señora Ramirez and Consuelo came to a standstill and stood like two monuments, staring after him, while the lines brushed past them on either side.

Lilina was looking out of her window at some boys who were playing on the corner of the street under the street light. One of them kept pulling a snake out of his pocket; he would then stuff it back in again. Lilina wanted the snake very much. She chose her toys according to the amount of power or responsibility she thought they would give her in the eyes of others. She thought now that if she were able to get the snake, she would perhaps put on a little act called "Lilina and the Viper", and charge admission. She imagined that she would wear a fancy dress and let the snake wriggle under her collar. She left her room and went out of doors. The wind was stronger than it had been, and she could hear the music playing even from where she was. She felt chilly and hurried toward the boys.

'For how much will you sell your snake?' she asked the oldest boy, Ramón.

'You mean Victoria?' said Ramón. His voice was beginning to change and there was a shadow above his upper lip.

'Victoria is too much of a queen for you to have,' said one of the smaller boys. 'She is a beauty and you are not.' They all roared with laughter, including Ramón, who all at once looked very silly. He giggled like a girl. Lilina's heart sank. She was determined to have the snake.

'Are you ever going to stop laughing and begin to bargain with me? If you don't I'll have to go back in, because my mother and sister will be coming home soon, and they wouldn't allow me to be talking here like this with you. I'm from a good family.'

This sobered Ramón, and he ordered the boys to be quiet. He took Victoria from his pocket and played with her in silence. Lilina stared at the snake.

'Come to my house,' said Ramón. 'My mother will want to know how much I'm selling her for.'

'All right,' said Lilina. 'But be quick, and I don't

want them with us.' She indicated the other boys. Ramón gave them orders to go back to their houses and meet him later at the playground near the Cathedral.

'Where do you live?' she asked him.

'Calle de las Delicias number six.'

'Does your house belong to you?'

'My house belongs to my Aunt Gudelia.'

'Is she richer than your mother?'

'Oh, yes.' They said no more to each other.

There were eight rooms opening onto the *patio* of Ramón's house, but only one was furnished. In this room the family cooked and slept. His mother and his aunt were seated opposite one another on two brightly painted chairs. Both were fat and both were wearing black. The only light came from a charcoal fire which was burning in a brazier on the floor.

They had bought the chairs that very morning and were consequently feeling light-hearted and festive. When the children arrived they were singing a little song together.

'Why don't we buy something to drink?' said Gudelia, when they stopped singing.

'Now you're going to go crazy, I see,' said Ramón's mother. 'You're very disagreeable when you're drinking.'

'No, I'm not,' said Gudelia.

'Mother,' said Ramón. 'This little girl has come to buy Victoria.'

'I have never seen you before,' said Ramón's mother to Lilina.

'Nor I,' said Gudelia. 'I am Ramón's aunt, Gudelia. This is my house.'

'My name is Lilina Ramirez. I want to bargain for Ramón's Victoria.'

'Victoria,' they repeated gravely.

'Ramón is very fond of Victoria and so are Gudelia and I,' said his mother. 'It's a shame that we sold Alfredo the parrot. We sold him for far too little. He sang and danced. We have taken care of Victoria for a long time, and it has been very expensive. She eats much meat.' This was an obvious lie. They all looked at Lilina.

'Where do you live, dear?' Gudelia asked Lilina.

'I live in the capital, but I'm staying now at Señora Espinoza's pension.'

'I meet her in the market every day of my life,' said Gudelia. 'Maria de la Luz Espinoza. She buys a lot. How many people has she staying in her house? Five, six?'

'Nine.'

'Nine! Dear God! Does she have many animals?'

'Certainly,' said Lilina.

'Come,' said Ramón to Lilina. 'Let's go outside and bargain.'

'He loves that snake,' said Ramón's mother, looking fixedly at Lilina.

The aunt sighed. 'Victoria . . . Victoria.'

Lilina and Ramón climbed through a hole in the wall and sat down together in the midst of some foliage.

'Listen,' said Ramón. 'If you kiss me, I'll give you Victoria for nothing. You have blue eyes. I saw them when we were in the street.'

'I can hear what you are saying,' his mother called out from the kitchen.

'Shame, shame,' said Gudelia. 'Giving Victoria away for nothing. Your mother will be without food. I can buy my own food, but what will your mother do?'

Lilina jumped to her feet impatiently. She saw that they were getting nowhere, and unlike most of her countrymen, she was always eager to get things done quickly.

She stamped back into the kitchen, opened her eyes very wide in order to frighten the two ladies, and shouted as loud as she could: 'Sell me that snake right now or I will go away and never put my foot in this house again.'

The two women were not used to such a display of rage over the mere settlement of a price. They rose from their chairs and started moving about the room to no purpose, picking up things and putting them down again. They were not quite sure what to do. Gudelia was terribly upset. She stepped here and there with her hand below her breast, peering about cautiously. Finally she slipped out into the *patio* and disappeared.

Ramón took Victoria out of his pocket. They arranged a price and Lilina left, carrying her in a little box.

Meanwhile Señora Ramirez and her daughter were on their way home from the band concert. Both of them were in a bad humour. Consuelo was not disposed to talk at all. She looked angrily at the houses they were passing and sighed at everything her mother had to say.

'You have no merriment in your heart,' said Señora Ramirez. 'Just revenge.' As Consuelo refused to answer, she continued. 'Sometimes I feel that I am walking along with an assassin.'

She stopped still in the street and looked up at the sky. '*Jesus Maria!*' she said. 'Don't let me say such things about my own daughter.' She clutched at Consuelo's arm.

'Come, come. Let us hurry. My feet ache. What an ugly city this is!'

Consuelo began to whimper. The word assassin had affected her painfully. Although she had no very clear idea of an assassin in her mind, she knew it to be a gross insult and contrary to all usage when applied to a young lady of breeding. It so frightened her that her mother had used such a word in connection with her, that she actually felt a little sick to her stomach.

'No, Mamá, no!' she cried. 'Don't say that I am an assassin. Don't!' Her hands were beginning to shake, and already the tears were filling her eyes. Her mother hugged her and they stood for a moment locked in each other's arms.

Maria, the servant, was standing near the fountain looking into it when Consuelo and her mother arrived at the pension. The traveller and Señorita Córdoba were seated together having a chat.

'Doesn't love interest you?' the traveller was asking her.

'No . . . no . . .' answered Señorita Córdoba. 'City life, business, the theatre. . . .' She sounded somewhat half-hearted about the theatre.

'Well, that's funny,' said the traveller. 'In my country most young girls are interested in love. There are some, of course, who are interested in having a career, either business or the stage. But I've heard tell that even these women deep down in their hearts want a home and everything that goes with it.'

'So?' said Señorita Córdoba.

'Well, yes,' said the traveller. 'Deep down in your heart don't you always hope the right man will come along some day?'

'No . . . no . . . no. . . . Do you?' she said absent-mindedly.

'Who, me? No.'

'No?'

She was the most preoccupied woman he had ever spoken with.

'Look, Señoras,' said Maria to Consuelo and her

mother. 'Look what is floating around in the fountain! What is it?'

Consuelo bent over the basin and fished around a bit. Presently she pulled out her mother's pink corset.

'Why, Mamá,' she said. 'It's your corset.'

Señora Ramirez examined the wet corset. It was covered with muck from the bottom of the fountain. She went over to a chair and sat down in it, burying her face in her hands. She rocked back and forth and sobbed very softly. Señora Espinoza came out of her room.

'Lilina, my sister, threw it into the fountain,' Consuelo announced to all present.

Señora Espinoza looked at the corset.

'It can be fixed. It can be fixed,' she said, walking over to Señora Ramirez and putting her arms around her.

'Look, my friend. My dear little friend, why don't you go to bed and get some sleep? Tomorrow you can think about getting it cleaned.'

'How can we stand it? Oh, how can we stand it?' Señora Ramirez asked imploringly, her beautiful eyes filled with sorrow. 'Sometimes,' she said in a trembling voice, 'I have no more strength than a sparrow. I would like to send my children to the four winds and sleep and sleep and sleep.'

Consuelo, hearing this, said in a gentle tone: 'Why don't you do so, Mamá?'

'They are like two daggers in my heart, you see?' continued her mother.

'No, they are not,' said Señora Espinoza. 'They are flowers that brighten your life.' She removed her glasses and polished them on her blouse.

'Daggers in my heart,' repeated Señora Ramirez.

'Have some hot soup,' urged Señora Espinoza. 'Maria will make you some—a gift from me—and then you can go to bed and forget all about this.'

'No, I think I will just sit here, thank you.'

'Mamá is going to have one of her fits,' said Consuelo to the servant. 'She does sometimes. She gets just like a child instead of getting angry, and she doesn't worry about what she is eating or when she goes to sleep, but she just sits in a chair or goes walking and her face looks very different from the way it looks at other times.' The servant nodded, and Consuelo went in to bed.

'I have French blood,' Señora Ramirez was saying to Señora Espinoza. 'I am very delicate for that reason —too delicate for my husband.'

Señora Espinoza seemed worried by the confession of her friend. She had no interest in gossip or in what people had to say about their lives. To Señora Ramirez she was like a man, and she often had dreams about her in which she became a man.

The traveller was highly amused.

'I'll be damned!' he said. 'All this because of an old corset. Some people have nothing to think about in this world. It's funny, though, funny as a barrel of monkeys.'

To Señorita Córdoba it was not funny. 'It's too bad,' she said. 'Very much too bad that the corset was spoiled. What are you doing here in this country?'

'I'm buying textiles. At least, I was, and now I'm just taking a little vacation here until the next boat leaves for the United States. I kind of miss my family and I'm anxious to get back. I don't see what you're supposed to get out of travelling.'

'Oh, yes, yes. Surely you do,' said Señorita Córdoba politely. 'Now if you will excuse me I am going inside to do a little drawing. I must not forget how in this peasant land.'

'What are you, an artist?' he asked.

'I draw dresses.' She disappeared.

'Oh, God!' thought the traveller after she had left. 'Here I am, left alone, and I'm not sleepy yet. This empty *patio* is so barren and so uninteresting, and as far as Señorita Córdoba is concerned, she's an iceberg. I like her neck though. She has a neck like a swan, so long and white and slender, the kind of neck you dream about girls having. But she's more like a virgin than a swan.' He turned around and noticed that Señora Ramirez was still sitting in her chair. He picked up his own chair and carried it over next to hers.

'Do you mind?' he asked. 'I see that you've decided to take a little night air. It isn't a bad idea. I don't feel like going to bed much either.'

'No,' she said. 'I don't want to go to bed. I will sit here. I like to sit out at night, if I am warmly enough dressed, and look up at the stars.'

'Yes, it's a great source of peace,' the traveller said. 'People don't do enough of it these days.'

'Would you not like very much to go to Italy?' Señora Ramirez asked him. 'The fruit trees and the flowers will be wonderful there at night.'

'Well, you've got enough fruit and flowers here, I should say. What do you want to go to Italy for? I'll bet there isn't as much variety in the fruit there as here.'

'No? Do you have many flowers in your country?'

The traveller was not able to decide.

'I would like really,' continued Señora Ramirez, 'to be somewhere else—in your country or in Italy. I would like to be somewhere where the life is beautiful. I care very much whether life is beautiful or ugly. People who live here don't care very much. Because they do not think.' She touched her finger to her forehead. 'I love beautiful things: beautiful houses, beautiful gardens, beautiful songs. When I was a young girl I was truly wild with happiness—doing and thinking and running in and out. I was so happy that my mother was afraid I would fall and break my leg or have some kind of accident. She was a very religious woman, but when I was a young girl I could not remember to think about such a thing. I was up always every morning before anybody except the Indians, and every morning I would go to market with them to buy food for all the houses. For many years I was doing this. Even when I was very little. It was very easy for me to do anything. I loved to learn English. I had a professor and I used to get on my knees in front of my father that the professor would stay longer with me every day. I was walking in the parks when my sisters were sleeping. My eyes were so big.' She made a circle with two fingers. 'And shiny like two diamonds, I was so excited all the time.' She churned the air with her clenched fist. 'Like this,' she said. 'Like a storm. My sisters called me wild Sofia. At the same time they were calling me wild Sofia, I was in love with my uncle, Aldo Torres. He never came much to the house before, but I heard my mother say that he had no more money and we would feed him. We were very rich and getting richer every year. I felt very sorry for him and was thinking about him all the time. We fell in love with each other and were kissing and hugging each other when nobody was there who could see us. I would have lived with him in a grass hut. He married a woman who had a little money, who also loved him very much. When he was married he got fat and started joking a lot with my father. I was glad for him that he was richer but pretty sad for myself. Then my sister Juanita, the oldest, married a very rich man. We were all very happy about her and there was a very big wedding.'

'You must have been broken-hearted though about

your uncle Aldo Torres going off with someone else, when you had befriended him so much when he was poor.'

'Oh, I liked him very much,' she said. Her memory seemed suddenly to have failed her and she did not appear to be interested in speaking any longer of the past. The traveller felt disturbed.

'I would love to travel,' she continued, 'very, very much, and I think it would be very nice to have the life of an actress, without children. You know it is my nature to love men and kissing.'

'Well,' said the traveller, 'nobody gets as much kissing as they would like to get. Most people are frustrated. You'd be surprised at the number of people in my country who are frustrated and good-looking at the same time.'

She turned her face toward his. The one little light bulb shed just enough light to enable him to see into her beautiful eyes. The tears were still wet on her lashes and they magnified her eyes to such an extent that they appeared to be almost twice their normal size. While she was looking at him she caught her breath.

'Oh, my darling man,' she said to him suddenly. 'I don't want to be separated from you. Let's go where I can hold you in my arms.' The traveller was feeling excited. She had taken hold of his hand and was crushing it very hard.

'Where do you want to go?' he asked stupidly.

'Into your bed.' She closed her eyes and waited for him to answer.

'All right. Are you sure?'

She nodded her head vigorously.

'This,' he said to himself, 'is undoubtedly one of those things that you don't want to remember next morning. I'll want to shake it off like a dog shaking water off its back. But what can I do? It's too far along now. I'll be going home soon and the whole thing will be just a soap bubble among many other soap bubbles.'

He was beginning to feel inspired and he could not understand it, because he had not been drinking.

'A soap bubble among many other soap bubbles,' he repeated to himself. His inner life was undefined but well controlled as a rule. Together they went into his room.

'Ah,' said Señora Ramirez, after he had closed the door behind them, 'this makes me happy.'

She fell onto the bed sideways, like a beaten person. Her feet stuck out into the air, and her heavy breathing filled the room. He realized that he had never before seen a person behave in this manner unless sodden with alcohol, and he did not know what to do. According to all his standards and the standards of his friends she was not a pleasant thing to lie beside.

She was unfastening her dress at the neck. The brooch with which she pinned her collar together she stuck into the pillow behind her.

'So much fat,' she said. 'So much fat.' She was

smiling at him very tenderly. This for some reason excited him, and he took off his own clothing and got into bed beside her. He was as cold as a clam and very bony, but being a truly passionate woman she did not notice any of that.

'Do you really want to go through with this?' he said to her, for he was incapable of finding new words for a situation that was certainly unlike any other he had ever experienced. She fell upon him and felt his face and his neck with feverish excitement.

'Dear God!' she said. 'Dear God!' They were in the very act of making love. 'I have lived twenty years for this moment and I cannot think that heaven itself could be more wonderful.'

The traveller hardly listened to this remark. His face was hidden in the pillow and he was feeling the pangs of guilt in the very midst of his pleasure. When it was all over she said to him: 'That is all I want to do ever.' She patted his hands and smiled at him.

'Are you happy, too?' she asked him.

'Yes, indeed,' he said. He got off the bed and went out into the *patio*.

'She was certainly in a bad way,' he thought. 'It was almost like death itself.' He didn't want to think any further. He stayed outside near the fountain as long as possible. When he returned she was up in front of the bureau trying to arrange her hair.

'I'm ashamed of the way I look,' she said. 'I don't look the way I feel.' She laughed and he told her that she looked perfectly all right. She drew him down onto the bed again. 'Don't send me back to my room,' she said. 'I love to be here with you, my sweetheart.'

The dawn was breaking when the traveller awakened next morning. Señora Ramirez was still beside him, sleeping very soundly. Her arm was flung over the pillow behind her head.

'Lordy,' said the traveller to himself. 'I'd better get her out of here.' He shook her as hard as he could.

'Mrs Ramirez,' he said. 'Mrs Ramirez, wake up. Wake up!' When she finally did wake up, she looked frightened to death. She turned and stared at him blankly for a little while. Before he noticed any change in her expression, her hand was already moving over his body.

'Mrs Ramirez,' he said. 'I'm worried that perhaps your daughters will get up and raise a hullabaloo. You know, start whining for you, or something like that. Your place is probably in there.'

'What?' she asked him. He had pulled away from her to the other side of the bed.

'I say I think you ought to go into your room now the morning's here.'

'Yes, my darling, I will go to my room. You are right.' She sidled over to him and put her arms around him.

'I will see you later in the dining-room, and look at you and look at you, because I love you so much.'

'Don't be crazy,' he said. 'You don't want anything

to show in your face. You don't want people to guess about this. We must be cold with one another.'

She put her hand over her heart.

'Ay!' she said. 'This cannot be.'

'Oh, Mrs Ramirez. Please be sensible. Look, you go to your room and we'll talk about this in the morning . . . or, at least, later in the morning.'

'Cold I cannot be.' To illustrate this, she looked deep into his eyes.

'I know, I know,' he said. 'You're a very passionate woman. But my God! Here we are in a crazy Spanish country.'

He jumped from the bed and she followed him. After she had put on her shoes, he took her to the door.

'Good-bye,' he said.

She couched her cheek on her two hands and looked up at him. He shut the door.

She was too happy to go right to bed, and so she went over to the bureau and took from it a little stale sugar Virgin which she broke into three pieces. She went over to Consuelo and shook her very hard. Consuelo opened her eyes, and after some time asked her mother crossly what she wanted. Señora Ramirez stuffed the candy into her daughter's mouth.

'Eat it, darling,' she said. 'It's the little Virgin from the bureau.'

'Ay, Mamá!' Consuelo sighed. 'Who knows what you will do next? It is already light out and you are still in your clothes. I am sure there is no other mother who is still in her clothes now, in the whole world. Please don't make me eat any more of the Virgin now. Tomorrow I will eat some more. But it is tomorrow, isn't it? What a mix-up. I don't like it.' She shut her eyes and tried to sleep. There was a look of deep disgust on her face. Her mother's spell was a little frightening this time.

Señora Ramirez now went over to Lilina's bed and awakened her. Lilina opened her eyes wide and immediately looked very tense, because she thought she was going to be scolded about the corset and also about having gone out alone after dark.

'Here, little one,' said her mother. 'Eat some of the Virgin.'

Lilina was delighted. She ate the stale sugar candy and patted her stomach to show how pleased she was. The snake was asleep in a box near her bed.

'Now tell me,' said her mother. 'What did you do today?' She had completely forgotten about the corset. Lilina was beside herself with joy. She ran her fingers along her mother's lips and then pushed them into her mouth. Señora Ramirez snapped at the fingers like a dog. Then she laughed uproarously.

'Mamá, please be quiet,' pleaded Consuelo. 'I want to go to sleep.'

'Yes, darling. Everything will be quiet so that you can sleep peacefully.'

'I bought a snake, Mamá,' said Lilina.

'Good!' exclaimed Señora Ramirez. And after musing a little while with her daughter's hand in hers, she went to bed.

In her room Señora Ramirez was dressing and talking to her children.

'I want you to put on your *fiesta* dresses,' she said, 'because I am going to ask the traveller to have lunch with us.'

Consuelo was in love with the traveller by now and very jealous of Señorita Córdoba, who she had decided was his sweetheart. 'I daresay he has already asked Señorita Córdoba to lunch,' she said. 'They have been talking together near the fountain almost since dawn.'

'*Santa Catarina!*' cried her mother angrily. 'You have the eyes of a madman who sees flowers where there are only cow turds.' She covered her face heavily with a powder that was distinctly violet in tint, and pulled a green chiffon scarf around her shoulders, pinning it together with a brooch in the form of a golf club. Then she and the girls, who were dressed in pink satin, went out into the *patio* and sat together just a little out of the sun. The parrot was swinging back and forth on his perch and singing. Señora Ramirez sang along with him; her own voice was a little lower than the parrot's.

'Pastores, pastores, vamos a Belen
A ver a Maria y al niño tambien.'

She conducted the parrot with her hand. The old Señora, mother of Señora Espinoza, was walking round and round the *patio*. She stopped for a moment and played with Señora Ramirez's seashell bracelet.

'Do you want some candy?' she asked Señora Ramirez.

'I can't. My stomach is very bad.'

'Do you want some candy?' she repeated. Señora Ramirez smiled and looked up at the sky. The old lady patted her cheek.

'Beautiful,' she said. 'You are beautiful.'

'Mamá!' screamed Señora Espinoza, running out of her room. 'Come to bed!'

The old lady clung to the rungs of Señora Ramirez's chair like a tough bird, and her daughter was obliged to pry her hands open before she was able to get her away.

'I'm sorry, Señora Ramirez,' she said. 'But when you get old, you know how it is.'

'Pretty bad,' said Señora Ramirez. She was looking at the traveller and Señorita Córdoba. They had their backs turned to her.

'Lilina,' she said. 'Go and ask him to have lunch with us . . . go. No, I will write it down. Get me a pen and paper.'

'Dear,' she wrote, when Lilina returned. 'Will you come to have lunch at my table this afternoon? The girls will be with me, too. All the three of us send you our deep affection. I tell Consuelo to tell the maid to move the plates all to the same table. Very truly yours, Sophia Piega de Ramirez.'

The traveller read the note, acquiesced, and shortly they were all seated together at the dining-room table.

'Now this is really stranger than fiction,' he said to himself. 'Here I am sitting with these people at their table and feeling as though I had been here all my life, and the truth of the matter is that I have only been in this pension about fourteen or fifteen hours altogether—not even one day. Yesterday I felt that I was on a Zulu island, I was so depressed. The human animal is the funniest animal of them all.'

Señora Ramirez had arranged to sit close beside the stranger, and she pressed her thigh to his all during the time that she was eating her soup. The traveller's appetite was not very good. He was excited and felt like talking.

After lunch Señora Ramirez decided to go for a walk instead of taking a *siesta* with her daughters. She put on her gloves and took with her an umbrella to shield her from the sun. After she had walked a little while she came to a long road, completely desolate save for a few ruins and some beautiful tall trees along the way. She looked about her and shook her head at the thought of the terrible earthquake that had thrown to the ground this city, reputed to have been once the most beautiful city in all the Western Hemisphere. She could see ahead of her, way at the road's end, the volcano named Fire. She crossed herself and bit her lips. She had come walking with the intention of dreaming of her lover, but the thought of this volcano which had erupted many centuries ago chased all dreams of love from her mind. She saw in her mind the walls of the houses caving in, and the roofs falling on the heads of the babies . . . and the mothers, their skirts covered with mud, running through the streets in despair.

'The innocents,' she said to herself. 'I am sure that God had a perfect reason for this, but what could it have been? *Santa Maria*, but what could it have been! If such a disorder should happen again on this earth, I would turn completely to jelly like a helpless idiot.'

She looked again at the volcano ahead of her, and although nothing had changed, to her it seemed that a cloud had passed across the face of the sun.

'You are crazy,' she went on, 'to think that an earthquake will again shake this city to the earth. You will not be going through such a trial as these other mothers went through because everything now is different. God doesn't send such big trials any more, like floods over the whole world, and plagues.'

She thanked her stars that she was living now and not before. It made her feel quite weak to think of the women who had been forced to live before she was born. The future too, she had heard, was to be very stormy because of wars.

'Ay!' she said to herself. 'Precipices on all sides of me!' It had not been such a good idea to take a walk, after all. She thought again of the traveller, shutting her eyes for a moment.

'*Mi amante! Amante querido!*' she whispered; and she remembered the little books with their covers lettered in gold, books about love, which she had read when she was a young girl, and without the burden of a family. These little books had made the ability to read seem like the most worthwhile and delightful talent to her. They had never, of course, touched on the coarser aspects of love, but in later years she did not find it strange that it was for such physical ends that the heroes and heroines had been pining. Never had she found any difficulty in associating nosegays and couplets with the more gross manifestations of love.

She turned off into another road in order to avoid facing the volcano, constantly ahead of her. She thought of the traveller without really thinking of him at all. Her eyes glowed with the pleasure of being in love and she decided that she had been very stupid to think of an earthquake on the very day that God was making a bed of roses for her.

'Thank you, thank you,' she whispered to Him, 'from the bottom of my heart. Ah!' She smoothed her dress over her bosom. She was suddenly very pleased with everything. Ahead she noticed that there was a very long convent, somewhat ruined, in front of which some boys were playing. There was also a little pavilion standing not far away. It was difficult to understand why it was so situated, where there was no formal park, nor any trees or grass—just some dirt and a few bushes. It had the strange static look of a ship that has been grounded. Señora Ramirez looked at it distastefully; it was a small kiosk anyway and badly in need of a coat of paint. But feeling tired, she was soon climbing up the flimsy steps, red in the face with fear lest she fall through to the ground. Inside the kiosk she spread a newspaper over the bench and sat down. Soon all her dreams of her lover faded from her mind, and she felt hot and fretful. She moved her feet around on the floor impatiently at the thought of having to walk all the way home. The dust rose up into the air and she was obliged to cover her mouth with her handkerchief.

'I wish to Heaven,' she said to herself, 'that he would come and carry me out of this kiosk.' She sat idly watching the boys playing in the dirt in front of the convent. One of them was a good deal taller than the others. As she watched their games, her head slumped forward and she fell asleep.

No tourists came, so the smaller boys decided to go over to the main square and meet the buses, to sell their lollipops and picture postcards. The oldest boy announced that he would stay behind.

'You're crazy,' they said to him. 'Completely crazy.'

He looked at them haughtily and did not answer. They ran down the road, screaming that they were going to earn a thousand *quetzales*.

He had remained behind because for some time he had noticed that there was someone in the kiosk. He knew even from where he stood that it was a woman because he could see that her dress was brightly coloured like a flower garden. She had been sitting there for a long time and he wondered if she were not dead.

'If she is dead,' he thought, 'I will carry her body all the way into town.' The idea excited him and he approached the pavilion with bated breath. He went inside and stood over Señora Ramirez, but when he saw that she was quite old and fat and obviously the mother of a good rich family he was frightened and all his imagination failed him. He thought he would go away, but then he decided differently, and he shook her foot. There was no change. Her mouth which had been open, remained so, and she went on sleeping. The boy took a good piece of the flesh on her upper arm between his thumb and forefinger and twisted it very hard. She awakened with a shudder and looked up at the boy perplexed.

His eyes were soft.

'I awakened you,' he said, 'because I have to go home to my house, and you are not safe here. Before, there was a man here in the bandstand trying to look under your skirt. When you are asleep, you know, people just go wild. There were some drunks here too, singing an obscene song, standing on the ground, right under you. You would have had red ears if you had heard it. I can tell you that.' He shrugged his shoulders and spat on the floor. He looked completely disgusted.

'What is the matter?' Señora Ramirez asked him.

'Bah! This city makes me sick. I want to be a carpenter in the capital, but I can't. My mother gets lonesome. All my brothers and sisters are dead.'

'Ay!' said Señora Ramirez. 'How sad for you! I have a beautiful house in the capital. Maybe my husband would let you be a carpenter there, if you did not have to stay with your mother.'

The boy's eyes were shining.

'I'm coming back with you,' he said. 'My uncle is with my mother.'

'Yes,' said Señora Ramirez. 'Maybe it will happen.'

'My sweetheart is there in the city,' he continued. 'She was living here before.'

Señora Ramirez took the boy's long hand in her own. The word sweetheart had recalled many things to her.

'Sit down, sit down,' she said to him. 'Sit down here beside me. I too have a sweetheart. He's in his room now.'

'Where does he work?'

'In the United States.'

'What luck for you! My sweetheart wouldn't love him better than she loves me, though. She wants me or simply death. She says so any time I ask her. She would tell the same thing to you if you asked her about me. It's the truth.'

Señora Ramirez pulled him down onto the bench next to her. He was confused and looked out over his shoulder at the road. She tickled the back of his hand and smiled up at him in a coquettish manner. The boy looked at her and his face seemed to weaken.

'You have blue eyes,' he said.

Señora Ramirez could not wait another minute. She took his head in her two hands and kissed him several times full on the mouth.

'Oh, God!' she said. The boy was delighted with her fine clothes, her blue eyes and her womanly ways. He took Señora Ramirez in his arms with real tenderness.

'I love you,' he said. Tears filled his eyes and because he was so full of a feeling of gratitude and kindness, he added: 'I love my sweetheart and I love you too.'

He helped her down the steps of the kiosk, and with his arm around her waist he led her to a sequestered spot belonging to the convent grounds.

The traveller was lying on his bed, consumed by a feeling of guilt. He had again spent the night with Señora Ramirez, and he was wondering whether or not his mother would read this in his eyes when he returned. He had never done anything like this before. His behaviour until now had never been without precedent, and he felt like a two-headed monster, as though he had somehow slipped from the real world into the other world, the world that he had always imagined as a little boy to be inhabited by assassins and orphans, and children whose mothers went to work. He put his head in his hands and wondered if he could ever forget Señora Ramirez. He remembered having read that the careers of many men had been ruined by women who because they had a certain physical stranglehold over them made it impossible for them to get away. These women, he knew, were always bad, and they were never Americans. Nor, he was certain, did they resemble Señora Ramirez. It was terrible to have done something he was certain none of his friends had ever done before him, nor would do after him. This experience, he knew, would have to remain a secret, and nothing made him feel more ill than having a secret. He liked to imagine that he and the group of men whom he considered to be his friends, discoursed freely on all things that were in their hearts and in their souls. He was beginning to talk to women in this free way, too—he talked to them a good deal, and he urged his friends to do likewise. He realized that he and Señora Ramirez never spoke, and this horrified him. He shuddered and said to himself: 'We are like two gorillas.'

He had been, it is true, with one or two prostitutes, but he had never taken them to his own bed, nor had he stayed with them longer than an hour. Also, they had been curly-headed blonde American girls recommended to him by his friends.

'Well,' he told himself, 'there is no use making

myself into a nervous wreck. What is done is done, and anyway, I think I might be excused on the grounds that: one, I am in a foreign country which has sort of put me off my balance; two, I have been eating strange foods that I am not used to, and living at an unusually high altitude for me; and, three, I haven't had my own kind to talk to for three solid weeks.'

He felt quite a good deal happier after having enumerated these extenuating conditions, and he added: 'When I get onto my boat I shall wave goodbye to the dock, and say good riddance to bad rubbish, and if the boss ever tries to send me out of the country, I'll tell him: "Not for a million dollars!"' He wished that it were possible to change pensions, but he had already paid for the remainder of the week. He was very thrifty, as, indeed, it was necessary for him to be. Now he lay down again on his bed, quite satisfied with himself, but soon he began to feel guilty again, and like an old truck horse, laboriously he went once more through the entire process of reassuring himself.

Lilina had put Victoria into a box and was walking in the town with her. Not far from the central square there was a dry-goods shop owned by a Jewish woman. Lilina had been there several times with her mother to buy wool. She knew the son of the proprietress, with whom she often stopped to talk. He was very quiet, but Lilina liked him. She decided to drop in at the shop now with Victoria.

When she arrived, the boy's mother was behind the counter stamping some old bolts of material with purple ink. She saw Lilina and smiled brightly.

'Enrique is in the *patio*. How nice of you to come and see him. Why don't you come more often?' She was very eager to please Lilina, because she knew the extent of Señora Ramirez's wealth and was proud to have her as a customer.

Lilina went over to the little door that led into the *patio* behind the shop, and opened it. Enrique was crouching in the dirt beside the washtubs. She was surprised to see that his head was wrapped in bandages. From a distance the dirty bandages gave the effect of a white turban.

She went a little nearer, and saw that he was arranging some marbles in a row.

'Good morning, Enrique,' she said to him.

Enrique recognized her voice, and without turning his head, he started slowly to pick up the marbles one at a time and put them into his pocket.

His mother had followed Lilina into the *patio*. When she saw that Enrique, instead of rising to his feet and greeting Lilina, remained absorbed in his marbles, she walked over to him and gave his arm a sharp twist.

'Leave those damned marbles alone and speak to Lilina,' she said to him. Enrique got up and went over to Lilina, while his mother, bending over with difficulty, finished picking up the marbles he had left behind on the ground.

Lilina looked at the big, dark red stain on Enrique's bandage. They both walked back into the store. Enrique did not enjoy being with Lilina. In fact, he was a little afraid of her. Whenever she came to the shop he could hardly wait for her to leave.

He went over now to a bolt of printed material which he started to unwind. When he had unwound a few yards, he began to follow the convolutions of the pattern with his index finger. Lilina, not realizing that his gesture was a carefully disguised insult to her, watched him with a certain amount of interest.

'I have something with me inside this box,' she said after a while.

Enrique, hearing his mother's footsteps approaching, turned and smiled at her sadly.

'Please show it to me,' he said.

She lifted the lid from the snake's box and took it over to Enrique.

'This is Victoria,' she said.

Enrique thought she was beautiful. He lifted her from her box and held her just below the head very firmly. Then he raised his arm until the snake's eyes were on a level with his own.

'Good morning, Victoria,' he said to her. 'Do you like it here in the store?'

This remark annoyed his mother. She had slipped down to the other end of the counter because she was terrified of the snake.

'You speak as though you were drunk,' she said to

Enrique. 'That snake can't understand a word you're saying.'

'She's really beautiful,' said Enrique.

'Let's put her back in the box and take her to the square,' said Lilina. But Enrique did not hear her, he was so enchanted with the sensation of holding Victoria.

His mother again spoke up. 'Do you hear Lilina talking to you?' she shouted. 'Or is that bandage covering your ears as well as your head?'

She had meant this remark to be stinging and witty, but she realized herself that there had been no point to it.

'Well, go with the little girl,' she added.

Lilina and Enrique set off toward the square together. Lilina had put Victoria back into her box.

'Why are we going to the square?' Enrique asked Lilina.

'Because we are going there with Victoria.'

Six or seven buses had converged in one of the streets that skirted the square. They had come from the capital and from other smaller cities in the region. The passengers who were not going any farther had already got out and were standing in a bunch talking together and buying food from the vendors. One lady had brought with her a cardboard fan intended as an advertisement for beer. She was fanning not only herself, but anyone who happened to come near her.

The bus drivers were racing their motors, and some were trying to move into positions more advantageous for departing. Lilina was excited by the noise and the crowd. Enrique, however, had sought a quiet spot, and was now standing underneath a tree. After a while she ran over to him and told him that she was going to let Victoria out of her box.

'Then we'll see what happens,' she said.

'No, no!' insisted Enrique. 'She'll only crawl under the buses and be squashed to death. Snakes live in the woods or in the rocks.'

Lilina paid little attention to him. Soon she was crouching on the edge of the kerbstone, busily unfastening the string around Victoria's box.

Enrique's head had begun to pain him and he felt a little ill. He wondered if he could leave the square, but he decided he did not have the courage. Although the wind had risen, the sun was very hot, and the tree afforded him little shade. He watched Lilina for a little while, but soon he looked away from her, and began to think instead about his own death. He was certain that his head hurt more today than usual. This caused him to sink into the blackest gloom, as he did whenever he remembered the day he had fallen and pierced his skull on a rusty nail. His life had always been precious to him, as far back as he could recall, and it seemed perhaps even more so now that he realized it could be violently interrupted. He disliked Lilina; probably because he suspected intuitively that she was a person who could fall over and over again into the same pile of broken glass and scream just as loudly the last time as the first.

By now Victoria had wriggled under the buses and been crushed flat. The buses cleared away, and Enrique was able to see what had happened. Only the snake's head, which had been severed from its body, remained intact.

Enrique came up and stood beside Lilina. 'Now are you going home?' he asked her, biting his lip.

'Look how small her head is. She must have been a very small snake,' said Lilina.

'Are you going home to your house?' he asked her again.

'No. I'm going over by the cathedral and play on the swings. Do you want to come? I'm going to run there.'

'I can't run,' said Enrique, touching his fingers to the bandages. 'And I'm not sure that I want to go over to the playground.'

'Well,' said Lilina. 'I'll run ahead of you and I'll be there if you decide to come.'

Enrique was very tired and a little dizzy, but he decided to follow her to the playground in order to ask her why she had allowed Victoria to escape under the buses.

When he arrived, Lilina was already swinging back and forth. He sat on a bench near the swings and looked up at her. Each time her feet grazed the ground, he tried to ask her about Victoria, but the question stuck in his throat. At last he stood up, thrust his hands into his pockets, and shouted at her.

'Are you going to get another snake?' he asked. It was not what he had intended to say. Lilina did not answer, but she did stare at him from the swing. It was impossible for him to tell whether or not she had heard his question.

At last she dug her heel into the ground and brought the swing to a standstill. 'I must go home,' she said, 'or my mother will be angry with me.'

'No,' said Enrique, catching hold of her dress. 'Come with me and let me buy you an ice.'

'I will,' said Lilina. 'I love them.'

They sat together in a little store, and Enrique bought two ices.

'I'd like to have a swing hanging from the roof of my house,' said Lilina. 'And I'd have my dinner and my breakfast served while I was swinging.' This idea amused her and she began to laugh so hard that her ice ran out of her mouth and over her chin.

'Breakfast, lunch and dinner and take a bath in the swing,' she continued. 'And make *pipi* on Consuelo's head from the swing.'

Enrique was growing more and more nervous because it was getting late, and still they were not talking about Victoria.

'Could I swing with you in your house?' he asked Lilina.

'Yes. We'll have two swings and you can make *pipi* on Consuelo's head, too.'

'I'd love to,' he said.

His question seemed more and more difficult to present. By now it seemed to him that it resembled more a declaration of love than a simple question.

Finally he tried again. 'Are you going to buy another snake?' But he still could not ask her why she had been so careless.

'No,' said Lilina. 'I'm going to buy a rabbit.'

'A rabbit?' he said. 'But rabbits aren't as intelligent or as beautiful as snakes. You had better buy another snake like Victoria.'

'Rabbits have lots of children,' said Lilina. 'Why don't we buy a rabbit together?'

Enrique thought about this for a while. He began to feel almost lighthearted, and even a little wicked.

'All right,' he said. 'Let's buy two rabbits, a man and a woman.' They finished their ices and talked together more and more excitedly about the rabbits.

On the way home, Lilina squeezed Enrique's hand and kissed him all over his cheeks. He was red with pleasure.

At the square they parted, after promising to meet again that afternoon.

It was a cloudy day, rather colder than usual, and Señora Ramirez decided to dress in her mourning clothes, which she always carried with her. She hung several strands of black beads around her neck and powdered her face heavily. She and Consuelo began to walk slowly around the *patio*.

Consuelo blew her nose. 'Ay, Mamá,' she said. 'Isn't it true that there is a greater amount of sadness in the world than happiness?'

'I don't know why you are thinking about this,' said her mother.

'Because I have been counting my happy days and my sad days. There are many more sad days, and I am living now at the best age for a girl. There is nothing but fighting, even at balls. I would not believe any man if he told me he liked dancing better than fighting.'

'This is true,' said her mother. 'But not all men are really like this. There are some men who are as gentle as little lambs. But not so many.'

'I feel like an old lady. I think that maybe I will feel better when I'm married.' They walked slowly past the traveller's door.

'I'm going inside,' said Consuelo suddenly.

'Aren't you going to sit in the *patio*?' her mother asked her.

'No, with all those children screaming and the chickens and the parrot talking and the white dog. And it's such a terrible day. Why?'

Señora Ramirez could not think of any reason why Consuelo should stay in the *patio*. In any case she preferred to be there alone if the stranger should decide to talk to her.

'What white dog?' she said.

'Señora Espinoza has bought a little white dog for the children.'

The wind was blowing and the children were chasing each other around the back *patio*. Señora Ramirez sat down on one of the little straight-backed chairs with her hands folded in her lap. The thought came into her mind that most days were likely to be cold and windy rather than otherwise, and that there would be many days to come exactly like this one. Unconsciously she had always felt that these were the days preferred by God, although they had never been much to her own liking.

The traveller was packing with the vivacity of one who is in the habit of making little excursions away from the charmed fold to return almost immediately.

'Wow!' he said joyfully to himself. 'I sure have been giddy in this place, but the bad dream is over now.' It was nearly bus time. He carried his bags out to the *patio*, and was confused to find Señora Ramirez sitting there. He prompted himself to be pleasant.

'Señora,' he said, walking over to her. 'It's good-bye now till we meet again.'

'What do you say?' she asked.

'I'm taking the twelve o'clock bus. I'm going home.'

'Ah! You must be very happy to go home.' She

did not think of looking away from his face. 'Do you take a boat?' she asked, staring harder.

'Yes. Five days on the boat.'

'How wonderful that must be. Or maybe it makes you sick.' She put her hand over her stomach.

'I have never been seasick in my life.'

She said nothing to this.

He backed against the parrot swinging on its perch, and stepped forward again quickly as it leaned to bite him.

'Is there anyone you would like me to look up in the United States?'

'No. You will be coming back in not such a long time?'

'No, I don't think I will come back here again. Well. . . .' He put out his hand and she stood up. She was fairly impressive in her black clothes. He looked at the beads that covered her chest.

'Well, good-bye, Señora. I was very happy to have met you.'

'*Adios*, Señor, and may God protect you on your trip. You will be coming back maybe. You don't know.'

He shook his head and walked over to the Indian boy standing by his luggage. They went out into the street and the heavy door closed with a bang. Señora Ramirez looked around the *patio*. She saw Señorita Córdoba move away from the half-open bedroom door where she had been standing.

CAMP CATARACT

Beryl knocked on Harriet's cabin door and was given permission to enter. She found her friend seated near the window, an open letter in her hand.

'Good evening, Beryl,' said Harriet. 'I was just reading a letter from my sister.' Her fragile, spinsterish face wore a canny yet slightly hysterical expression.

Beryl, a stocky blonde waitress with stubborn eyes, had developed a dogged attachment to Harriet and sat in her cabin whenever she had a moment to spare. She rarely spoke in Harriet's presence, nor was she an attentive listener.

'I'll read you what she says; have a seat.' Harriet indicated a straight chair and Beryl dragged it into a dark corner where she sat down. It creaked dangerously under the weight of her husky body.

'Hope I don't bust the chair,' said Beryl, and she blushed furiously, digging her hands deep into the pockets of the checked plus-fours she habitually wore when she was not on duty.

' "Dear Sister," ' Harriet read. ' "You are still at Camp Cataract visiting the falls and enjoying them. I always want you to have a good time. This is your fifth week away. I suppose you go on standing behind the falls with much enjoyment like you told me all the guests did. I think you said only the people who don't stay overnight have to pay to stand behind the waterfall . . . you stay ten weeks . . . have a nice time, dear. Here everything is exactly the same as when you left. The apartment doesn't change. I have something I want to tell you, but first let me say that if you get nervous, why don't you come home instead of waiting until you are no good for the train trip? Such a thing could happen. I wonder of course how you feel about the apartment once you are by the waterfall. Also, I want to put this to you. Knowing that you have an apartment and a loving family must make Camp Cataract quite a different place than it would be if it were all the home and loving you had. There must be wretches like that up there. If you see them, be sure to give them loving because they are the lost souls of the earth. I fear nomads. I am afraid of them and afraid for them too. I don't know what I would do if any of my dear ones were seized with the wanderlust. We are meant to cherish those who through God's will are given into our hands. First of all come the members of the family, and for this it is better to live as close as possible. Maybe you would say, 'Sadie is old-fashioned; she doesn't want people to live on their own.' I am not old-fashioned, but I don't want any of us to turn into nomads. You don't grow rich in spirit by widening your circle but by tending your own. When you are gone, I get afraid about you. I think that you might be seized with the wanderlust and that you are not remembering the apartment very much. Particularly this trip . . . but then I know this cannot be true and that only my nerves make me think such things. It's so hot out. This is a record-breaking summer. Remember, the apartment is not just a row of rooms. It is the material proof that our spirits are so wedded that we have but one blessed roof over our heads. There are only three of us in the apartment related by blood, but Bert Hoffer has joined the three through the normal channels of marriage, also sacred. I know that you feel this way too about it and that just nerves makes me think Camp Cataract can change anything. May I remind you also that if this family is a garland, you are the middle flower; for me you are anyway. Maybe Evy's love is now flowing more to Bert Hoffer because he's her husband, which is natural. I wish they didn't think you needed to go to Camp Cataract because of your spells. Haven't I always tended you when you had them? Bert's always taken Evy to the Hoffers and we've stayed together, just the two of us, with the door safely locked so you wouldn't in your excitement run to a neighbour's house at all hours of the morning. Evy liked going to the Hoffers because they always gave her chicken with dumplings or else goose with red cabbage. I hope you haven't got it in your head that just because you are an old maid you have to go somewhere and be by yourself. Remember, I am also an old maid. I must close now, but I am not satisfied with my letter because I have so much more to say. I know you love the apartment and feel the way I feel. You are simply getting a tourist's thrill out of being there in a cabin like all of us do. I count the days until your sweet return. Your loving sister, Sadie." '

Harriet folded the letter. 'Sister Sadie,' she said to Beryl, 'is a great lover of security.'

'She sounds swell,' said Beryl, as if Harriet were mentioning her for the first time, which was certainly not the case.

'I have no regard for it whatsoever,' Harriet announced in a positive voice. '*None*. In fact, I am a great admirer of the nomad, vagabonds, gypsies, seafaring men. I tip my hat to them; the old prophets roamed the world for that matter too, and most of the visionaries.' She folded her hands in her lap with an air of satisfaction. Then, clearing her throat as if for a public address, she continued. 'I don't give a tinker's damn about feeling part of a community, I can assure you. . . . That's not why I stay on at the apartment . . . not for a minute, but it's a good reason why she does . . . I mean Sadie; she loves a community spirit and she loves us all to be in the apartment because the apartment is in the community. She can get an actual thrill out of knowing that. But of course I can't . . . I never could, never in a thousand years.'

She tilted her head back and half closed her eyes. In the true style of a person given to interminable monologues, she was barely conscious of her audience. 'Now,' she said, 'we can come to whether I, on the other hand, get a thrill out of Camp Cataract.' She paused for a moment as if to consider this. 'Actually, I don't,' she pronounced sententiously, 'but if you like, I will clarify my statement by calling Camp Cataract my *tree house*. You remember tree houses from your younger days. . . . You climb into them when you're a child and plan to run away from home once you are safely hidden among the leaves. They're popular with children. Suppose I tell you point-blank that I'm an extremely original woman, but also a very shallow one . . . in a sense, a *very* shallow one. I am afraid of scandal.' Harriet assumed a more erect position. 'I despise anything that smacks of a bohemian dash for freedom; I know that this has nothing to do with the more serious things in life . . . I'm sure there are hundreds of serious people who kick over their traces and jump into the gutter; but I'm too shallow for anything like that . . . I know it and I enjoy knowing it. Sadie on the other hand cooks and cleans all day long and yet takes her life as seriously as she would a religion . . . myself and the apartment and the Hoffers. By the Hoffers, I mean my sister Evy and her big pig of a husband Bert.' She made a wry face. 'I'm the only one with taste in the family but I've never even suggested a lamp for the apartment. I wouldn't lower myself by becoming involved. I do however refuse to make an unseemly dash for freedom. I refuse to be known as "Sadie's wild sister Harriet". There is something intensely repulsive to me about unmarried women setting out on their own . . . also a very shallow attitude. You may wonder how a woman can be shallow and know it at the same time, but then, this is precisely the tragedy of any person, if he allows himself to be griped.' She paused for a moment and looked into the darkness with a fierce light in her eyes. 'Now let's get back to Camp Cataract,' she said with renewed vigour. 'The pine groves, the canoes, the sparkling purity of the brook water and cascade . . . the cabins . . . the marshmallows, the respectable clientele.'

'Did you ever think of working in a garage?' Beryl suddenly blurted out, and then she blushed again at the sound of her own voice.

'No,' Harriet answered sharply. 'Why should I?'

Beryl shifted her position in her chair. 'Well,' she said, 'I think I'd like that kind of work better than waiting on tables. Especially if I could be boss and own my garage. It's hard, though, for a woman.'

Harriet stared at her in silence. 'Do you think Camp Cataract smacks of the gutter?' she asked a minute later.

'No, sir. . . .' Beryl shook her head with a woeful air.

'Well then, there you have it. It is, of course, the farthest point from the gutter that one could reach. Any blockhead can see that. My plan is extremely complicated and from my point of view rather brilliant. First I will come here for several years . . . I don't know yet exactly how many, but long enough to imitate roots . . . I mean to imitate the natural family roots of childhood . . . long enough so that I myself will feel: "Camp Cataract is *habit*, Camp Cataract is life, Camp Cataract is not escape." Escape is unladylike, habit isn't. As I remove myself gradually from within my family circle and establish myself more and more solidly into Camp Cataract, then from here at some later date I can start making my sallies into the outside world almost unnoticed. None of it will seem to the onlooker like an ugly impetuous escape. I intend to rent the same cabin every year and to stay a little longer each time. Meanwhile I'm learning a great deal about trees and flowers and bushes . . . I am interested in nature.' She was quiet for a moment. 'It's rather lucky too,' she added, 'that the doctor has approved of my separating from the family for several months out of every year. He's a blockhead and doesn't remotely suspect the extent of my scheme nor how perfectly he fits into it . . . in fact, he has even sanctioned my request that no one visit me here at the camp. I'm afraid if Sadie did, and she's the only one who would dream of it, I wouldn't be able to avoid a wrangle and then I might have a fit. The fits are unpleasant; I get much more nervous than I usually am and there's a blank moment or two.' Harriet glanced sideways at Beryl to see how she was reacting to this last bit of information, but Beryl's face was impassive.

'So you see my plan,' she went on, in a relaxed, offhand manner; 'complicated, a bit dotty and completely original . . . but then, I *am* original . . . not like my sisters . . . oddly enough I don't even seem to belong socially to the same class as my sisters do. I am somehow'—she hesitated for a second—'more fashionable.'

Harriet glanced out of the window. Night had fallen during the course of her monologue and she could see a light burning in the next cabin. 'Do you think I'm a coward?' she asked Beryl.

The waitress was startled out of her torpor. Fortunately her brain registered Harriet's question as well. 'No, sir,' she answered. 'If you were, you wouldn't go out paddling canoes solo, with all the scary shoots you run into up and down these rivers. . . .'

Harriet twisted her body impatiently. She had a sudden and uncontrollable desire to be alone. 'Goodbye,' she said rudely. 'I'm not coming to supper.'

Beryl rose from her chair. 'I'll save something for you in case you get hungry after the dining room's closed. I'll be hanging around the lodge like I always am till bedtime.' Harriet nodded and the waitress stepped out of the cabin, shutting the door carefully behind her so that it would not make any noise.

Harriet's sister Sadie was a dark woman with loose features and sad eyes. She was turning slightly to fat in her middle years, and did not in any way resemble Harriet, who was only a few years her senior. Ever since she had written her last letter to Harriet about Camp Cataract and the nomads Sadie had suffered from a feeling of steadily mounting suspense—the suspense itself a curious mingling of apprehension and thrilling anticipation. Her appetite grew smaller each day and it was becoming increasingly difficult for her to accomplish her domestic tasks.

She was standing in the parlour gazing with blank eyes at her new furniture set—two enormous easy chairs with bulging arms and a sofa in the same style—when she said aloud: 'I can talk to her better than I can put it in a letter.' Her voice had been automatic and when she heard her own words a rush of unbounded joy flooded her heart. Thus she realized that she was going on a little journey to Camp Cataract. She often made important decisions this way, as if some prearranged plot were being suddenly revealed to her, a plot which had immediately to be concealed from the eyes of others, because for Sadie, if there was any problem implicit in making a decision, it lay, not in the difficulty of choosing, but in the concealment of her choice. To her, secrecy was the real absolution from guilt, so automatically she protected all of her deepest feelings and compulsions from the eyes of Evy, Bert Hoffer and the other members of the family, although she had no interest in understanding or examining these herself.

The floor shook; recognizing Bert Hoffer's footsteps, she made a violent effort to control the flux of her blood so that the power of her emotion would not be reflected in her cheeks. A moment later her brother-in-law walked across the room and settled in one of the easy chairs. He sat frowning at her for quite a little while without uttering a word in greeting, but Sadie had long ago grown accustomed to his unfriendly manner; even in the beginning it had not upset her too much because she was such an obsessive that she was not very concerned with outside details.

'God-damned velours,' he said finally. 'It's the hottest stuff I ever sat on.'

'Next summer we'll get covers,' Sadie reassured him, 'with a flower pattern if you like. What's your favourite flower?' she asked, just to make conversation and to distract him from looking at her face.

Bert Hoffer stared at her as if she'd quite taken leave of her senses. He was a fat man with a red face and wavy hair. Instead of answering this question, which he considered idiotic, he mopped his brow with his handkerchief.

'I'll fix you a canned pineapple salad for supper,' she said to him with glowing eyes. 'It will taste better than heavy meat on a night like this.'

'If you're going to dish up pineapple salad for supper,' Bert Hoffer answered with a dark scowl, 'you can telephone some other guy to come and eat it. You'll find me over at Martie's Tavern eating meat and potatoes, if there's any messages to deliver.'

'I thought because you were hot,' said Sadie.

'I was talking about the velvet wasn't I? I didn't say anything about the meat.'

He was a very trying man indeed, particularly in a small apartment, but Sadie never dwelled upon this fact at all. She was delighted to cook and clean for him and for her sister Evelyn so long as they consented to live under the same roof with her and Harriet.

Just then Evelyn walked briskly into the parlour. Like Sadie she was dark, but here the resemblance ceased, for she had a small and wiry build, with a flat chest, and her hair was as straight as an Indian's. She stared at her husband's shirt sleeves and at Sadie's apron with distaste. She was wearing a crisp summer dress with a very low neckline, an unfortunate selection for one as bony and fierce-looking as she.

'You both look ready for the dump heap, not for the dining room,' she said to them. 'Why do we bother to have a dining room . . . is it just a farce?'

'How was the office today?' Sadie asked her sister.

Evelyn looked at Sadie and narrowed her eyes in closer scrutiny. The muscles in her face tightened. There was a moment of dead silence, and Bert Hoffer, cocking a wary eye in his wife's direction, recognized the dangerous flush on her cheeks. Secretly he was pleased. He loved to look on when Evelyn blew up at Sadie, but he tried to conceal his enjoyment because he did not consider it a very masculine one.

'What's the matter with you?' Evelyn asked finally, drawing closer to Sadie. 'There's something wrong besides your dirty apron.'

Sadie coloured slightly but said nothing.

'You look crazy,' Evelyn yelled. 'What's the matter with you? You look so crazy I'd be almost afraid to ask you to go to the store for something. Tell me what's happened!' Evelyn was very excitable; nonetheless hers was a strong and sane nature.

'I'm not crazy,' Sadie mumbled. 'I'll go get the dinner.' She pushed slowly past Evelyn and with her heavy step she left the parlour.

The mahogany dining table was much too wide for the small oblong-shaped room, clearing the walls comfortably only at the two ends. When many guests were present some were seated first on one side of the room and were then obliged to draw the table toward themselves, until its edge pressed painfully into their diaphragms, before the remaining guests could slide into their seats on the opposite side.

Sadie served the food, but only Bert Hoffer ate with any appetite. Evelyn jabbed at her meat once or twice, tasted it, and dropped her fork, which fell with a clatter on to her plate.

Had the food been more savoury she might not have pursued her attack on Sadie until later, or very likely she would have forgotten it altogether. Unfortunately, however, Sadie, although she insisted on fulfilling the role of housewife, and never allowed the others to acquit themselves of even the smallest domestic task, was a poor cook and a careless cleaner as well. Her lumpy gravies were tasteless, and she had once or twice boiled a good cut of steak out of indifference. She was lavish, too, in spite of being indifferent, and kept her cupboards so loaded with food that a certain quantity spoiled each week and there was often an unpleasant odour about the house. Harriet, in fact, was totally unaware of Sadie's true nature and had fallen into the trap her sister had instinctively prepared for her, because beyond wearing an apron and simulating the airs of other housewives, Sadie did not possess a community spirit at all, as Harriet had stated to Beryl the waitress. Sadie certainly yearned to live in the grown-up world that her parents had established for them when they were children, but in spite of the fact that she had wanted to live in that world with Harriet, and because of Harriet, she did not understand it properly. It remained mysterious to her even though she did all the housekeeping and managed the apartment entirely alone. She couldn't ever admit to herself that she lived in constant fear that Harriet would go away, but she brooded a great deal on outside dangers, and had she tried, she could not have remembered a time when this fear had not been her strongest emotion.

Sometimes an ecstatic and voracious look would come into her eyes, as if she would devour her very existence because she loved it so much. Such passionate moments of appreciation were perhaps her only reward for living a life which she knew in her heart was one of perpetual narrow escape. Although Sadie was neither sly nor tricky, but on the contrary profoundly sincere and ingenuous, she schemed unconsciously to keep the Hoffers in the apartment with them, because she did not want to reveal the true singleness of her interest either to Harriet or to herself. She sensed as well that Harriet would find it more difficult to break away from all three of them (because as a group they suggested a little society, which impressed her sister) than she would to escape from her alone. In spite of her mortal dread that Harriet might strike out on her own, she had never brooded on the possibility of her sister's marrying. Here, too, her instinct was correct: she knew that she was safe and referred often to the 'normal channels of marriage', conscious all the while that such an intimate relationship with a man would be as uninteresting to Harriet as it would to herself.

From a financial point of view this communal living worked out more than satisfactorily. Each sister had inherited some real estate which yielded her a small monthly stipend; these stipends, combined with the extra money that the Hoffers contributed out of their salaries, covered their common living expenses. In return for the extra sum the Hoffers gave toward the household expenses Sadie contributed her work, thus saving them the money they would have spent hiring a servant, had they lived alone. A fourth sister, whose marriage had proved financially more successful than Evy's, contributed generously toward Harriet's support at Camp Cataract, since Harriet's stipend certainly did not yield enough to cover her share of their living expenses at the apartment and pay for a long vacation as well.

Neither Sadie nor Bert Hoffer had looked up when Evy's fork clattered onto her plate. Sadie was truly absorbed in her own thoughts, whereas Bert Hoffer was merely pretending to be, while secretly he rejoiced at the unmistakable signal that his wife was about to blow up.

'When I find out why Sadie looks like that if she isn't going to be crazy, then I'll eat,' Evelyn announced flatly, and she folded her arms across her chest.

'I'm not crazy,' Sadie said indistinctly, glancing toward Bert Hoffer, not in order to enlist his sympathies, but to avoid her younger sister's sharp scrutiny.

'There's a big danger of your going crazy because of Grandma and Harriet,' said Evelyn crossly. 'That's why I get so nervous the minute you look a little out of the way, like you do tonight. It's not that you get Harriet's expression . . . but then you might be getting a different kind of craziness . . . maybe worse. She's all right if she can go away and there's not too much excitement . . . it's only in spells anyway. But you —you might get a worse kind. Maybe it would be steadier.'

'I'm not going to be crazy,' Sadie murmured apologetically.

Evelyn glowered in silence and picked up her fork, but then immediately she let it fall again and turned on her sister with renewed exasperation. 'Why don't you ask me why *I'm* not going to be crazy?' she demanded. 'Harriet's my sister and Grandma's my grandma just as much as she is yours, isn't she?'

Sadie's eyes had a faraway look.

'If you were normal,' Evelyn pursued, 'you'd give me an intelligent argument instead of not paying any attention. Do you agree, Hoffer?'

'Yes, I do,' he answered soberly.

Evelyn stiffened her back. 'I'm too much like everybody else to be crazy,' she announced with pride. 'At a picture show, I feel like the norm.'

The technical difficulty of disappearing without announcing her plan to Evelyn suddenly occurred to Sadie, who glanced up quite by accident at her sister. She knew, of course, that Harriet was supposed to avoid contact with her family during these vacation months at the doctor's request and even at Harriet's own; but like some herd animal, who though threatened with the stick continues grazing, Sadie pursued her thoughts imperturbably. She did not really believe in Harriet's craziness nor in the necessity of her visits to Camp Cataract, but she was never in conscious opposition to the opinions of her sisters. Her attitude was rather like that of a child who is bored by the tedium of grown-up problems and listens to them with a vacant ear. As usual she was passionately concerned only with successfully dissimulating what she really felt, and had she been forced to admit openly that there existed such a remarkable split between her own opinions and those of her sisters, she would have suffered unbelievable torment. She was able to live among them, listening to their conferences with her dead outside ear (the more affluent sister was also present at these sessions, and her husband as well), and even to contribute a pittance toward Harriet's support at the camp, without questioning either the validity of their decisions or of her own totally divergent attitude. By a self-imposed taboo, awareness of this split was denied her, and she had never reflected upon it.

Harriet had gone to Camp Cataract for the first time a year ago, after a bad attack of nerves combined with a return of her pleurisy. It had been suggested by the doctor himself that she go with his own wife and child instead of travelling with one of her sisters.

Harriet had been delighted with the suggestion and Sadie had accepted it without a murmur. It was never her habit to argue, and in fact she had thought nothing of Harriet's leaving at the time. It was only gradually that she had begun writing the letters to Harriet about Camp Cataract, the nomads and the wanderlust—for she had written others similar to her latest one, but never so eloquent or full of conviction. Previous letters had contained a hint or two here and there, but had been for the main part factual reports about her summer life in the apartment. Since writing this last letter she had not been able to forget her own wonderful and solemn words (for she was rarely eloquent), and even now at the dinner table they rose continually in her throat so that she was thrilled over and over again and could not bother her head about announcing her departure to Evelyn. 'It will be easier to write a note,' she said to herself. 'I'll pack my valise and walk out tomorrow afternoon, while they're at business. They can get their own dinners for a few days. Maybe I'll leave a great big meat loaf.' Her eyes were shining like stars.

'Take my plate and put it in the warmer, Hoffer,' Evelyn was saying. 'I won't eat another mouthful until Sadie tells us what we can expect. If she feels she's going off, she can at least warn us about it. I deserve to know how she feels . . . I tell every single thing I feel to her and Harriet . . . I don't sneak around the house like a thief. In the first place I don't have any time for sneaking, I'm at the office all day! Is this the latest vogue, this sneaking around and hiding everything you can from your sister? Is it?' She stared at Bert Hoffer, widening her eyes in fake astonishment. He shrugged his shoulders.

'I'm no sneak or hypocrite and neither are you, Hoffer, you're no hypocrite. You're just sore at the world, but you don't pretend you love the world, do you?'

Sadie was lightheaded with embarrassment. She had blanched at Evy's allusion to her going, which she mistook naturally for a reference to her intention of leaving for Camp Cataract.

'Only for a few days . . .' she mumbled in confusion, 'and then I'll be right back here at the table.'

Evelyn looked at her in consternation. 'What do you mean by announcing calmly how many days it's going to be?' she shouted at her sister. 'That's really sacrilegious! Did you ever hear of such a crusty sacrilegious remark in your life before?' She turned to Bert Hoffer, with a horror-stricken expression on her face. 'How can I go to the office and look neat and clean and happy when this is what I hear at home . . . when my sister sits here and says she'll only go crazy for a few days? How *can* I go to the office after that? How can I look right?'

'I'm not going to be crazy,' Sadie assured her again in a sorrowful tone, because although she felt relieved that Evelyn had not, after all, guessed the truth, hers was not a nature to indulge itself in trivial glee at having put someone off her track.

'You just said you were going to be crazy,' Evelyn exclaimed heatedly. 'Didn't she, Bert?'

'Yes,' he answered, 'she did say something like that. . . .'

The tendons of Evelyn's neck were stretched tight as she darted her eyes from her sister's face to her husband's. 'Now, tell me this much,' she demanded, 'do I go to the office every day looking neat and clean or do I go looking like a bum?'

'You look OK,' Bert said.

'Then why do my sisters spit in my eye? Why do they hide everything from me if I'm so decent? I'm wide open, I'm frank, there's nothing on my mind besides what I say. Why can't they be like other sisters all over the world? One of them is so crazy that she must live in a cabin for her nerves at *my* expense, and the other one is planning to go crazy deliberately and behind my back.' She commenced to struggle out of her chair, which as usual proved to be a slow and labourious task. Exasperated, she shoved the table vehemently away from her toward the opposite wall. 'Why don't we leave the space all on one side when there's no company?' she screamed at both of them, for she was now annoyed with Bert Hoffer as well as with Sadie. Fortunately they were seated at either end of the table and so did not suffer as a result of her violent gesture, but the table jammed into four chairs ranged on the opposite side, pinning three of them backward against the wall and knocking the fourth onto the floor.

'Leave it there,' Evelyn shouted dramatically above the racket. 'Leave it there till doomsday,' and she rushed headlong out of the room.

They listened to her gallop down the hall.

'What about the dessert?' Bert Hoffer asked Sadie with a frown. He was displeased because Evelyn had spoken to him sharply.

'Leftover bread pudding without raisins.' She had just gotten up to fetch the pudding when Evelyn summoned them from the parlour.

'Come in here, both of you,' she hollered. 'I have something to say.'

They found Evelyn seated on the couch, her head tilted 'way back on a cushion, staring fixedly at the ceiling. They settled into easy chairs opposite her.

'I could be normal and light in any other family,' she said, 'I'm normally a gay light girl . . . not a morose one. I like all the material things.'

'What do you want to do tonight?' Bert Hoffer interrupted, speaking with authority. 'Do you want to be excited or do you want to go to the movies?' He was always bored by these self-appraising monologues which succeeded her explosions.

Evy looked as though she had not heard him, but after a moment or two of sitting with her eyes shut she got up and walked briskly out of the room; her husband followed her.

Neither of them had said good-bye to Sadie, who went over to the window as soon as they'd gone and looked down on the huge unsightly square below her. It was crisscrossed by trolley tracks going in every possible direction. Five pharmacies and seven cigar stores were visible from where she stood. She knew that modern industrial cities were considered ugly, but she liked them. 'I'm glad Evy and Bert have gone to a picture show.' Sadie remarked to herself after a while. 'Evy gets high-strung from being at the office all day.'

A little later she turned her back on the window and went to the dining-room.

'Looks like the train went through here,' she murmured, gazing quietly at the chairs tilted back against the wall and the table's unsightly angle; but the tumult in her breast had not subsided, even though she knew she was leaving for Camp Cataract. Beyond the first rush of joy she had experienced when her plan had revealed itself to her earlier, in the parlour, the feeling of suspense remained identical, a curious admixture of anxiety and anticipation, difficult to bear. Concerning the mechanics of the trip itself she was neither nervous nor foolishly excited. 'I'll call up tomorrow,' she said to herself, 'and find out when the buses go, or maybe I'll take the train. In the morning I'll buy three different meats for the loaf, if I don't forget. It won't go rotten for a few days, and even if it does they can eat at Martie's or else Evy will make bologna and eggs . . . she knows how, and so does Bert.' She was not really concentrating on these latter projects any more than she usually did on domestic details.

The lamp over the table was suspended on a heavy iron chain. She reached for the beaded string to extinguish the light. When she released it the massive lamp swung from side to side in the darkness.

'Would you like it so much by the waterfall if you didn't know the apartment was here?' she whispered into the dark, and she was thrilled again by the beauty of her own words. 'How much more I'll be able to say when I'm sitting right next to her,' she murmured almost with reverence. '. . . And then we'll come back here,' she added simply, not in the least startled to discover that the idea of returning with Harriet had been at the root of her plan all along.

Without bothering to clear the plates from the table, she went into the kitchen and extinguished the light there. She was suddenly overcome with fatigue.

When Sadie arrived at Camp Cataract it was raining hard.

'This shingled building is the main lodge,' the hack driver said to her. 'The ceiling in there is three times higher than average, if you like that style. Go up on the porch and just walk in. You'll get a kick out of it.'

Sadie reached into her pocketbook for some money.

'My wife and I come here to drink beer when we're

in the mood,' he continued, getting out his change. 'If there's nobody much inside, don't get panicky; the whole camp goes to the movies on Thursday nights. The wagon takes them and brings them back. They'll be along soon.'

After thanking him she got out of the cab and climbed the wooden steps on to the porch. Without hesitating she opened the door. The driver had not exaggerated; the room was indeed so enormous that it suggested a gymnasium. Wicker chairs and settees were scattered from one end of the floor to the other and numberless sawed-off tree stumps had been set down to serve as little tables.

Sadie glanced around her and then headed automatically for a giant fireplace, difficult to reach because of the accumulation of chairs and settees that surrounded it. She threaded her way between these and stepped across the hearth into the cold vault of the chimney, high enough to shelter a person of average stature. The andirons, which reached to her waist, had been wrought in the shape of witches. She fingered their pointed iron hats. 'Novelties,' she murmured to herself without enthusiasm. 'They must have been especially made.' Then, peering out of the fireplace, she noticed for the first time that she was not alone. Some fifty feet away a fat woman sat reading by the light of an electric bulb.

'She doesn't even know I'm in the fireplace,' she said to herself. 'Because the rain's so loud, she probably didn't hear me come in.' She waited patiently for a while and then, suspecting that the woman might remain oblivious to her presence indefinitely, she called over to her. 'Do you have anything to do with managing Camp Cataract?' she asked, speaking loudly so that she could be heard above the rain.

The woman ceased reading and switched her big light off at once, since the strong glare prevented her seeing beyond the radius of the bulb.

'No, I don't,' she answered in a booming voice. 'Why?'

Sadie, finding no answer to this question, remained silent.

'Do you think I look like a manager?' the woman pursued, and since Sadie had obviously no intention of answering, she continued the conversation by herself.

'I suppose you might think I was manager here, because I'm stout, and stout people have that look; also I'm about the right age for it. But I'm not the manager . . . I don't manage anything, anywhere. I have a domineering cranium all right, but I'm more the French type. I'd rather enjoy myself than give orders.'

'French . . .' Sadie repeated hesitantly.

'Not French,' the woman corrected her. 'French *type*, with a little of the actual blood.' Her voice was cold and severe.

For a while neither of them spoke, and Sadie hoped the conversation had drawn to a definite close.

'Individuality is my god,' the woman announced abruptly, much to Sadie's disappointment. 'That's partly why I didn't go to the picture show tonight. I don't like doing what the groups do, and I've seen the film.' She dragged her chair forward so as to be heard more clearly. 'The steadies here—we call the ones who stay more than a fortnight steadies—are all crazy to get into birds-of-a-feather-flock-together arrangements. If you look around, you can see for yourself how clubby the furniture is fixed. Well, they can go in for it, if they want, but I won't. I keep my chair out in the open here, and when I feel like it I take myself over to one circle or another . . . there's about ten or twelve circles. Don't you object to the confinement of a group?'

'We haven't got a group back home,' Sadie answered briefly.

'I don't go in for group worship either,' the woman continued, 'any more than I do for the heavy social mixing. I don't even go in for individual worship, for that matter. Most likely I was born to such a vigorous happy nature I don't feel the need to worry about what's up there over my head. I get the full flavour out of all my days whether anyone's up there or not. The groups don't allow for that kind of zip . . . never. You know what rotten apples in a barrel can do to the healthy ones.'

Sadie, who had never before met an agnostic, was profoundly shocked by the woman's blasphemous attitude. 'I'll bet she slept with a lot of men she wasn't married to when she was younger,' she said to herself.

'Most of the humanity you bump into is unhealthy and nervous,' the woman concluded, looking at Sadie with a cold eye, and then without further remarks she struggled out of her chair and began to walk towards a side door at the other end of the room. Just as she approached it the door was flung open from the other side by Beryl, whom the woman immediately warned of the new arrival. Beryl, without ceasing to spoon some beans out of a can she was holding, walked over to Sadie and offered to be of some assistance. 'I can show you rooms,' she suggested. 'Unless you'd rather wait till the manager comes back from the movies.'

When she realized, however, after a short conversation with Sadie, that she was speaking to Harriet's sister, a malevolent scowl darkened her countenance, and she spooned her beans more slowly.

'Harriet didn't tell me you were coming,' she said at length; her tone was unmistakably disagreeable.

Sadie's heart commenced to beat very fast as she in turn realized that this woman in plus-fours was the waitress, Beryl, of whom Harriet had often spoken in her letters and at home.

'It's a surprise,' Sadie told her. 'I meant to come here before. I've been promising Harriet I'd visit her in camp for a long time now, but I couldn't come until I got a neighbour in to cook for Evy and Bert. They're a husband and wife . . . my sister Evy and her husband Bert.'

'I know about those two,' Beryl remarked sullenly, 'Harriet's told me all about them.'

'Will you please take me to my sister's cabin?' Sadie asked, picking up her valise and stepping forward.

Beryl continued to stir her beans around without moving.

'I thought you folks had some kind of arrangement,' she said. She had recorded in her mind entire passages of Harriet's monologues out of love for her friend, although she felt no curiosity concerning the material she had gathered. 'I thought you folks were supposed to stay in the apartment while she was away at camp.'

'Bert Hoffer and Evy have never visited Camp Cataract,' Sadie answered in a tone that was innocent of any subterfuge.

'You bet they haven't,' Beryl pronounced triumphantly. 'That's part of the arrangement. They're supposed to stay in the apartment while she's here at camp; the doctor said so.'

'They're not coming up,' Sadie repeated, and she still wore, not the foxy look that Beryl expected would betray itself at any moment, but the look of a person who is attentive though being addressed in a foreign language. The waitress sensed that all her attempts at starting a scrap had been successfully blocked for the present and she whistled carefully, dragging some chairs into line with a rough hand. 'I'll tell you what,' she said, ceasing her activities as suddenly as she had begun them. 'Instead of taking you down there to the Pine Cones—that's the name of the grove where her cabin is—I'll go myself and tell her to come up here to the lodge. She's got some nifty rain equipment so she won't get wet coming through the groves like you would . . . lots of pine trees out there.'

Sadie nodded in silence and walked over to a fantasy chair where she sat down.

'They get a lot of fun out of that chair. When they're drunk,' said Beryl pointing to its back, made of a giant straw disc. 'Well . . . so long. . . .' She strode away. 'Dear Valley . . .' Sadie heard her sing as she went out the door.

Sadie lifted the top off the chair's left arm and pulled two books out of its woven hamper. The larger volume was entitled, *The Growth and Development of the Texas Oil Companies*, and the smaller, *Stories from Other Climes*. Hastily she replaced them and closed the lid.

Harriet opened the door for Beryl and quickly shut it again, but even in that instant the wooden flooring of the threshold was thoroughly soaked with rain. She was wearing a lavender kimono with a deep ruffle at the neckline; above it her face shone pale with dismay at Beryl's late and unexpected visit. She feared that perhaps the waitress was drunk. 'I'm certainly not hacking out a free place for myself in this world just in order to cope with drunks,' she said to herself with bitter verve. Her loose hair was hanging to her shoulders and Beryl looked at it for a moment in mute admiration before making her announcement.

'Your sister Sadie's up at the lodge,' she said, recovering herself; then, feeling embarrassed, she shuffled over to her usual seat in the darkest corner of the room.

'What are you saying?' Harriet questioned her sharply.

'Your sister Sadie's up at the lodge,' she repeated, not daring to look at her. 'Your sister Sadie who wrote you the letter about the apartment.'

'But she can't be!' Harriet screeched. 'She can't be! It was all arranged that no one was to visit me here.'

'That's what I told her,' Beryl put in.

Harriet began pacing up and down the floor. Her pupils were dilated and she looked as if she were about to lose all control of herself. Abruptly she flopped down on the edge of the bed and began gulping in great draughts of air. She was actually practising a system which she believed had often saved her from complete hysteria, but Beryl, who knew nothing about her method, was horrified and utterly bewildered. 'Take it easy,' she implored Harriet. 'Take it easy!'

'Dash some water in my face,' said Harriet in a strange voice, but horror and astonishment anchored Beryl securely to her chair, so that Harriet was forced to stagger over to the basin and manage by herself. After five minutes of steady dousing she wiped her face and chest with a towel and resumed her pacing. At each instant the expression on her face was more indignant and a trifle less distraught. 'It's the boorishness of it that I find so appalling,' she complained, a suggestion of theatricality in her tone which a moment before had not been present. 'If she's determined to wreck my schemes, why doesn't she do it with some style, a little slight bit of cunning? I can't picture anything more boorish than hauling oneself onto a train and simply chugging straight up here. She has no sense of scheming, of intrigue in the grand manner . . . none whatever. Anyone meeting only Sadie would think the family raised potatoes for a living. Evy doesn't make a much better impression, I must say. If they met her they'd decide we were all clerks! But at least she goes to business. . . . She doesn't sit around thinking about how to mess my life up all day. She thinks about Bert Hoffer. Ugh!' She made a wry face.

'When did you and Sadie start fighting?' Beryl asked her.

'I don't fight with Sadie,' Harriet answered, lifting her head proudly. 'I wouldn't dream of fighting like a common fishwife. Everything that goes on between us goes on undercover. It's always been that way. I've always hidden everything from her ever since I was a little girl. She's perfectly aware that I know she's trying to hold me a prisoner in the apartment out of plain jealousy and she knows too that I'm afraid of being considered a bum, and that makes matters simpler for her. She pretends to be worried that I might forget myself if I left the apartment and commit a folly with some man I wasn't married to, but actually she knows perfectly well that I'm as cold as ice. I haven't the slightest interest in men . . . nor in women either for that matter; still if I stormed out of the apartment dramatically the way some do, they might think I was a bum on my way to a man . . . and I won't give Sadie that satisfaction, ever. As for marriage, of course I admit I'm peculiar and there's a bit wrong with me, but even so I shouldn't want to marry: I think the whole system of going through life with a partner is repulsive in every way.' She paused, but only for a second. 'Don't you imagine, however,' she added severely, looking directly at Beryl, 'don't you imagine that just because I'm a bit peculiar and different from the others, that I'm not fussy about my life. I *am* fussy about it, and I *hate* a scandal.'

'To hell with sisters!' Beryl exclaimed happily. 'Give 'em all a good swift kick in the pants.' She had regained her own composure watching the colour return to Harriet's cheeks and she was just beginning to think with pleasure that perhaps Sadie's arrival would serve to strengthen the bond of intimacy between herself and Harriet, when this latter buried her head in her lap and burst into tears. Beryl's face fell and she blushed at her own frivolousness.

'I can't any more,' Harriet sobbed in anguished tones. 'I can't . . . I'm old . . . I'm much too old.' Here she collapsed and sobbed so pitifully that Beryl, wringing her hands in grief, sprang to her side, for she was a most tenderhearted person toward those whom she loved. 'You are not old . . . you are beautiful,' she said, blushing again, and in her heart she was thankful that Providence had granted her the occasion to console her friend in a grief-stricken moment, and to compliment her at the same time.

After a bit, Harriet's sobbing subsided, and jumping up from the bed, she grabbed the waitress. 'Beryl,' she gasped, 'you must run back to the lodge right away.' There was a beam of cunning in her tear-filled eyes.

'Sure will,' Beryl answered.

'Go back to the lodge and see if there's a room left up there, and if there is, take her grip into it so that there will be no question of her staying in my cabin. I can't have her staying in my cabin. It's the only place I have in the whole wide world.' The beam of cunning disappeared again and she looked at Beryl with wide, frightened eyes. '. . . And if there's no room?' she asked.

'Then I'll put her in my place,' Beryl reassured her. 'I've got a neat little cabin all to myself that she can have and I'll go bunk in with some dopey waitress.'

'Well, then,' said Harriet, 'go, and hurry! Take her grip to a room in the upper lodge annex or to your own cabin before she has a chance to say anything, and then come straight back here for me. I can't get through these pine groves alone . . . now . . . I know I can't.' It did not occur to her to thank Beryl for the kind offer she had made.

'All right,' said the waitress, 'I'll be back in a jiffy and don't you worry about a thing.' A second later she was lumbering through the drenched pine groves with shining eyes.

When Beryl came into the lodge and snatched Sadie's grip up without a word of explanation, Sadie did not protest. Opposite her there was an open staircase which led to a narrow gallery hanging halfway between the ceiling and the floor. She watched the waitress climbing the stairs, but once she had passed the landing Sadie did not trouble to look up and follow her progress around the wooden balcony overhead.

A deep chill had settled into her bones, and she was like a person benumbed. Exactly when this present state had succeeded the earlier one Sadie could not tell, nor did she think to ask herself such a question, but a feeling of dread now lay like a stone in her breast where before there had been stirring such powerful sensations of excitement and suspense. 'I'm so low,' she said to herself. 'I feel like I was sitting at my own funeral.' She did not say this in the spirit of hyperbolic gloom which some people nurture to work themselves out of a bad mood, but in all seriousness and with her customary attitude of passivity; in fact, she wore the humble look so often visible on the faces of sufferers who are being treated in a free clinic. It did not occur to her that a connection might exist between her present dismal state and the mission she had come to fulfill at Camp Cataract, nor did she take any notice of the fact that the words which were to enchant Harriet and accomplish her return were no longer welling up in her throat as they had done all the past week. She feared that something dreadful might happen, but whatever it was, this disaster was as remotely connected with her as a possible train wreck. 'I hope nothing bad happens . . .' she thought, but she didn't have much hope in her.

Harriet slammed the front door and Sadie looked up. For the first second or two she did not recognize the woman who stood on the threshold in her dripping rubber coat and hood. Beryl was beside her; puddles were forming around the feet of the two women. Harriet had rouged her cheeks rather more highly than usual in order to hide all traces of her crying spell. Her eyes were bright and she wore a smile that was fixed and hard.

'Not a night fit for man or beast,' she shouted across to Sadie, using a voice that she thought sounded hearty and yet fashionable at the same time; she did this, not in order to impress her sister, but to keep her at a safe distance.

Sadie, instead of rushing to the door, stared at her

with an air of perplexity. To her Harriet appeared more robust and coarse-featured than she had five weeks ago at the apartment, and yet she knew that such a rapid change of physiognomy was scarcely possible. Recovering, she rose and went to embrace her sister. The embrace failed to reassure her because of Harriet's wet rubber coat, and her feeling of estrangement became more defined. She backed away.

Upon hearing her own voice ring out in such hearty and fashionable tones, Harriet had felt crazily confident that she might, by continuing to affect this manner, hold her sister at bay for the duration of her visit. To increase her chances of success she had determined right then not to ask Sadie why she had come, but to treat the visit in the most casual and natural way possible.

'Have you put on fat?' Sadie asked, at a loss for anything else to say.

'I'll never be fat,' Harriet replied quickly, 'I'm a fruit lover, not a lover of starches.'

'Yes, you love fruit,' Sadie said nervously. 'Do you want some? I have an apple left from my lunch.'

Harriet looked aghast. 'Now!' she exclaimed. 'Beryl can tell you that I never eat at night; in fact I never come up to the lodge at night, *never*. I stay in my cabin. I've written you all about how early I get up . . . I don't know anything about the lodge at night,' she added almost angrily, as though her sister had accused her of being festive.

'You don't?' Sadie looked at her stupidly.

'No, I don't. Are you hungry, by the way?'

'If she's hungry,' put in Beryl, 'we can go into the Grotto Room and I'll bring her the food there. The tables in the main dining room are all set up for tomorrow morning's breakfast.'

'I despise the Grotto,' said Harriet with surprising bitterness. Her voice was getting quite an edge to it, and although it still sounded fashionable it was no longer hearty.

'I'm not hungry,' Sadie assured them both. 'I'm sleepy.'

'Well, then,' Harriet replied quickly, jumping at the opportunity, 'we'll sit here for a few minutes and then you must go to bed.'

The three of them settled in wicker chairs close to the cold hearth. Sadie was seated opposite the other two, who both remained in their rubber coats.

'I really do despise the Grotto,' Harriet went on; 'actually I don't hang around the lodge at all. This is not the part of Camp Cataract that interests me. I'm interested in the pine groves, my cabin, the rocks, the streams, the bridge, and all the surrounding natural beauty . . . the sky also.'

Although the rain still continued its drumming on the roof above them, to Sadie, Harriet's voice sounded intolerably loud, and she could not rid herself of the impression that her sister's face had grown fatter. 'Now,' she heard Harriet saying in her loud voice, 'tell me about the apartment. . . . What's new, how are the dinners coming along, how are Evy and Bert?'

Fortunately, while Sadie was struggling to answer these questions, which unaccountably she found it difficult to do, the stout agnostic reappeared, and Harriet was immediately distracted.

'Rover,' she called gaily across the room, 'come and sit with us. My sister Sadie's here.'

The woman joined them, seating herself beside Beryl so that Sadie was now facing all three.

'It's a surprise to see you up at the lodge at night, Hermit,' she remarked to Harriet without a spark of mischief in her voice.

'You see!' Harriet nodded at Sadie with immense satisfaction. 'I was not fibbing, was I? How are Evy and Bert?' she asked again, her face twitching a bit. 'Is the apartment hot?'

Sadie nodded.

'I don't know how long you plan to stay,' Harriet rattled on, feeling increasingly powerful and therefore reckless, 'but I'm going on a canoe trip the day after tomorrow for five days. We're going up the river to Pocahontas Falls. . . . I leave at four in the morning, too, which rather ruins tomorrow as well. I've been looking forward to this trip ever since last spring when I applied for my seat, back at the apartment. The canoes are limited, and the guides. . . . I'm devoted to canoe trips, as you know, and can fancy myself a redskin all the way to the Falls and back, easily.'

Sadie did not answer.

'There's nothing weird about it,' Harriet argued. 'It's in keeping with my hatred of industrialization. In any case, you can see what a chopped-up day tomorrow's going to be. I have to make my pack in the morning and I must be in bed by eight-thirty at night, the latest, so that I can get up at four. I'll have only one real meal, at two in the afternoon. I suggest we meet at two behind the souvenir booth; you'll notice it tomorrow.' Harriet waited expectantly for Sadie to answer in agreement to this suggestion, but her sister remained silent.

'Speaking of the booth,' said Rover, 'I'm not taking home a single souvenir this year. They're expensive and they don't last.'

'You can buy salt-water taffy at Gerald's Store in town,' Beryl told her. 'I saw some there last week. It's a little stale but very cheap.'

'Why would they sell salt-water taffy in the mountains?' Rover asked irritably.

Sadie was half listening to the conversation; as she sat watching them, all three women were suddenly unrecognizable; it was as if she had flung open the door to some dentist's office and seen three strangers seated there. She sprang to her feet in terror.

Harriet was horrified. 'What is it?' she yelled at her sister. 'Why do you look like that? Are you mad?'

Sadie was pale and beads of sweat were forming under her felt hat, but the women opposite her had already regained their correct relation to herself and the present moment. Her face relaxed, and although her legs were trembling as a result of her brief but shocking experience, she felt immensely relieved that it was all over.

'Why did you jump up?' Harriet screeched at her. 'Is it because you are at Camp Cataract and not at the apartment?'

'It must have been the long train trip and no food . . .' Sadie told herself, 'only one sandwich.'

'Is it because you are at Camp Cataract and not at the apartment?' Harriet insisted. She was really very frightened and wished to establish Sadie's fit as a purposeful one and not as an involuntary seizure similar to one of her one.

'It was a long and dirty train trip,' Sadie said in a weary voice. 'I had only one sandwich all day long, with no mustard or butter . . . just the processed meat. I didn't even eat my fruit.'

'Beryl offered to serve you food in the Grotto!' Harriet ranted. 'Do you want some now or not? For heaven's sake, speak up!'

'No . . . no.' Sadie shook her head sorrowfully. 'I think I'd best go to bed. Take me to your cabin . . . I've got my slippers and my kimono and my nightgown in my satchel,' she added, looking around her vaguely, for the fact that Beryl had carried her grip off had never really impressed itself upon her consciousness.

Harriet glanced at Beryl with an air of complicity

and managed to give her a quick pinch. 'Beryl's got you fixed up in one of the upper lodge annex rooms,' she told Sadie in a false, chatterbox voice. 'You'll be much more comfortable up here than you would be down in my cabin. We all use oil lamps in the grove and you know how dependent you are on electricity.'

Sadie didn't know whether she was dependent on electricity or not since she had never really lived without it, but she was so tired that she said nothing.

'I get up terribly early and my cabin's draughty, besides,' Harriet went on. 'You'll be much more comfortable here. You'd hate the Boulder Dam wigwams as well. Anyway, the wigwams are really for boys and they're always full. There's a covered bridge leading from this building to the annex on the upper floor, so that's an advantage.'

'OK, folks,' Beryl cut in, judging that she could best help Harriet by spurring them on to action. 'Let's get going.'

'Yes,' Harriet agreed, 'if we don't get out of the lodge soon the crowd will come back from the movies and we certainly want to avoid them.'

They bade good night to Rover and started up the stairs.

'This balustrade is made of young birch limbs,' Harriet told Sadie as they walked along the narrow gallery overhead. 'I think it's very much in keeping with the lodge, don't you?'

'Yes, I do,' Sadie answered.

Beryl opened the door leading from the balcony onto a covered bridge and stepped through it, motioning to the others. 'Here we go onto the bridge,' she said, looking over her shoulder. 'You've never visited the annex have you?' she asked Harriet.

'I've never had any reason to,' Harriet answered in a huffy tone. 'You know how I feel about my cabin.'

They walked along the imperfectly fitted boards in the darkness. Gusts of wind blew about their ankles and they were constantly spattered with rain in spite of the wooden roofing. They reached the door at the other end very quickly, however, where they descended two steps leading into a short, brightly lit hall. Beryl closed the door to the bridge behind them. The smell of fresh plaster and cement thickened the damp air.

'This is the annex,' said Beryl. 'We put old ladies here mostly, because they can get back and forth to the dining-room without going outdoors . . . and they've got the toilet right here, too.' She flung open the door and showed it to them. 'Then also,' she added, 'we don't like the old ladies dealing with oil lamps and here they've got electricity.' She led them into a little room just at their left and switched on the light. 'Pretty smart, isn't it?' she remarked, looking around her with evident satisfaction, as if she herself had designed the room; then, sauntering over to a modernistic wardrobe-bureau combination, she polished a corner of it with her pocket handkerchief. This piece was made of shiny brown wood and fitted with a rimless circular mirror. 'Strong and good-looking,' Beryl said, rapping on the wood with her knuckles. 'Every room's got one.'

Sadie sank down on the edge of the bed without removing her outer garments. Here, too, the smell of plaster and cement permeated the air, and the wind still blew about their ankles, this time from under the badly constructed doorsill.

'The cabins are much draughtier than this,' Harriet assured Sadie once again. 'You'll be more comfortable here in the annex.' She felt confident that establishing her sister in the annex would facilitate her plan, which was still to prevent her from saying whatever she had come to say.

Sadie was terribly tired. Her hat, dampened by the rain, pressed uncomfortably against her temples, but she did not attempt to remove it. 'I think I've got to go to sleep,' she muttered. 'I can't stay awake any more.'

'All right,' said Harriet, 'but don't forget tomorrow at two by the souvenir booth . . . you can't miss it. I don't want to see anyone in the morning because I can make my canoe pack better by myself . . . it's frightfully complicated. . . . But if I hurried I could meet you at one-thirty; would you prefer that?'

Sadie nodded.

'Then I'll do my best. . . . You see, in the morning I always practise imagination for an hour or two. It does me lots of good, but tomorrow I'll cut it short.' She kissed Sadie lightly on the crown of her felt hat.

'Good night,' she said, 'is there anything I forgot to ask you about the apartment?'

'No,' Sadie assured her. 'You asked everything.'

'Well, good night,' said Harriet once again, and followed by Beryl, she left the room.

When Sadie awakened the next morning a feeling of dread still rested like a leaden weight on her chest. No sooner had she left the room than panic, like a small wing, started to beat under her heart. She was inordinately fearful that if she strayed any distance from the main lodge she would lose her way and so arrive late for her meeting with Harriet. This fear drove her to stand next to the souvenir booth fully an hour ahead of time. Fortunately the booth, situated on a small knoll, commanded an excellent view of the cataract, which spilled down from some high rock ledges above a deep chasm. A fancy bridge spanned this chasm only a few feet below her, so that she was able to watch the people crossing it as they walked back and forth between the camp site and the waterfall. An Indian chief in full war regalia was seated at the bridge entrance on a kitchen chair. His magnificent feather head-dress curved gracefully in the breeze as he busied himself collecting the small toll that all the tourists paid on returning from the waterfall; he supplied them with change from a nickel-plated conductor's belt which he wore over his deer-hide jacket, embroidered with minute beads. He was an Irishman employed by the management, which supplied his costume. Lately he had grown careless, and often neglected to stain his freckled hands the deep brick colour of his face. He divided his time between the bridge and the souvenir booth, clambering up the knoll whenever he sighted a customer.

A series of wooden arches, Gothic in conception, succeeded each other all the way across the bridge; bright banners fluttered from their rims, each one stamped with the initials of the camp, and some of them edged with a glossy fringe. Only a few feet away lay the dining terrace, a huge flagstone pavilion whose entire length skirted the chasm's edge.

Unfortunately neither the holiday crowds, nor the festooned bridge, nor even the white waters of the cataract across the way could distract Sadie from her misery. She constantly glanced behind her at the dark pine groves wherein Harriet's cabin was concealed. She dreaded to see Harriet's shape define itself between the trees, but at the same time she feared that if her sister did not arrive shortly some terrible catastrophe would befall them both before she'd had a chance to speak. In truth all desire to convince her sister that she should leave Camp Cataract and return to the apartment had miraculously shrivelled away, and with the desire, the words to express it had vanished too. This did not in any way alter her intention of accomplishing her mission; on the contrary it seemed to her all the more desperately important now that she was almost certain, in her innermost heart, that her trip was already a failure. Her attitude was not an astonishing one, since like many others she conceived of her life as separate from herself; the road was laid out always a little ahead of her by sacred hands, and she walked down it without a question. This road, which was her life, would go on existing after her death, even as her death existed now while she still lived.

There were close to a hundred people dining on the terrace, and the water's roar so falsified the clamour of voices that one minute the guests seemed to be speaking from a great distance and the next right at her elbow. Every now and then she thought she heard someone pronounce her name in a dismal tone, and however much she told herself that this was merely the waterfall playing its tricks on her ears she shuddered each time at the sound of her name. Her very position next to the booth began to embarrass her. She tucked her hands into her coat sleeves so that they would not show, and tried to keep her eyes fixed on the foaming waters across the way, but she had noticed a disapproving look in the eyes of the diners nearest her, and she could not resist glancing back at the terrace every few minutes in the hope that she had been mistaken. Each time, however, she was more convinced that she had read their expressions correctly, and that these people believed, not only that she was standing there for no good reason, but that she was a genuine vagrant who could not afford the price of a dinner. She was therefore immensely relieved when she caught sight of Harriet advancing between the tables from the far end of the dining pavilion. As she drew nearer Sadie noticed that she was wearing her black winter coat trimmed with red fur, and that her marcelled hair remained neatly arranged in spite of the strong wind. Much to her relief Harriet had omitted to rouge her cheeks and her face therefore had regained its natural proportions. She saw Harriet wave at the sight of her and quicken her step. Sadie was pleased that the diners were to witness the impending meeting. 'When they see us together,' she thought, 'they'll realize that I'm no vagrant, but a decent woman visiting her sister.' She herself started down the knoll to hasten the meeting. 'I thought you'd come out of the pine grove,' she called out, as soon as they were within a few feet of one another. 'I kept looking that way.'

'I would have ordinarily,' Harriet answered, reaching her side and kissing her lightly on the cheek, 'but I went to the other end of the terrace first, to reserve a table for us from the waiter in charge there. That end is quieter, so it will be more suitable for a long talk.'

'Good,' thought Sadie as they climbed up the knoll together. 'Her night's sleep has done her a world of good.' She studied Harriet's face anxiously as they paused next to the souvenir booth, and discovered a sweet light reflected in her eyes. All at once she remembered their childhood together and the great tenderness Harriet had often shown towards her then.

'They have Turkish pilaff on the menu,' said Harriet, 'so I told the waiter to save some for you. It's such a favourite that it usually runs out at the very beginning. I know how much you love it.'

Sadie, realizing that Harriet was actually eager for this dinner, the only one they would eat together at Camp Cataract, to be a success, felt the terrible leaden weight lifted from her heart; it disappeared so suddenly that for a moment or two she was like a balloon without its ballast; she could barely refrain from dancing about in delight. Harriet tugged on her arm.

'I think we'd better go now,' she urged Sadie, 'then after lunch we can come back here if you want to buy some souvenirs for Evy and Bert . . . and maybe for Flo and Carl and Bobby too. . . .'

Sadie bent down to adjust her cotton stockings, which were wrinkling badly at the ankles, and when she straightened up again her eyes lighted on three men dining very near the edge of the terrace; she had not noticed them before. They were all eating corn on the cob and big round hamburger sandwiches in absolute silence. To protect their clothing from spattering kernels, they had converted their napkins into bibs.

'Bert Hoffer's careful of his clothes too,' Sadie reflected, and then she turned to her sister. 'Don't you think men look different sitting all by themselves without women?' she asked her. She felt an extraordinary urge to chat—an urge which she could not remember ever having experienced before.

'I think,' Harriet replied, as though she had not heard Sadie's comment, 'that we'd better go to our table before the waiter gives it to someone else.'

'I don't like men,' Sadie announced without venom, and she was about to follow Harriet when her attention was arrested by the eyes of the man nearest her. Slowly lowering his corn-cob to his plate, he stared across at her, his mouth twisted into a bitter smile. She stood as if rooted to the ground, and under his steady gaze all her new-born joy rapidly drained away. With desperation she realized that Harriet, darting in and out between the crowded tables, would soon be out of sight. After making what seemed to her a superhuman effort she tore herself away from the spot where she stood and lunged after Harriet shouting her name.

Harriet was at her side again almost instantly, looking up at her with a startled expression. Together they returned to the souvenir booth, where Sadie stopped and assumed a slightly bent position as if she were suffering from an abdominal pain.

'What's the trouble?' she heard Harriet asking with concern. 'Are you feeling ill?'

Instead of answering Sadie laid her hand heavily on her sister's arm and stared at her with a hunted expression in her eyes.

'Please try not to look so much like a gorilla,' said Harriet in a kind voice, but Sadie, although she recognized the accuracy of this observation (for she could feel very well that she was looking like a gorilla), was powerless to change her expression, at least for a moment or two. 'Come with me,' she said finally, grabbing Harriet's hand and pulling her along with almost brutal force. 'I've got something to tell you.'

She headed down a narrow path leading into a thickly planted section of the grove, where she thought they were less likely to be disturbed. Harriet followed with such a quick, light step that Sadie felt no pull behind her at all and her sister's hand, folded in her own thick palm, seemed as delicate as the body of a bird. Finally they entered a small clearing where they stopped. Harriet untied a handkerchief from around her neck and mopped her brow. 'Gracious!' she said. 'It's frightfully hot in here.' She offered the kerchief to Sadie. 'I suppose it's because we walked so fast and because the pine trees shut out all the wind. . . . First I'll sit down and then you must tell me what's wrong.' She stepped over to a felled tree whose length blocked the clearing. Its torn roots were shockingly exposed, whereas the upper trunk and branches lay hidden in the surrounding grove. Harriet sat down; Sadie was about to sit next to her when she noticed a dense swarm of flies near the roots. Automatically she stepped toward them. 'Why are they here?' she asked herself—then immediately she spotted the cause, an open can of beans some careless person had deposited inside a small hollow at the base of the trunk. She turned away in disgust and looked at Harriet. Her sister was seated on the fallen tree, her back gracefully erect and her head tilted in a listening attitude. The filtered light imparted to her face an incredibly fragile and youthful look, and Sadie gazed at her with tenderness and wonder. No sound reached them in the clearing, and she realized with a pounding heart that she could no longer postpone telling Harriet why she had come. She could not have wished for a moment more favourable to the accomplishment of her purpose. The stillness in the air, their isolation, the expectant and gentle light in Harriet's eye, all these elements should have combined to give her back her faith—faith in her own powers to persuade Harriet to come home with her and live among them once again, winter and summer alike, as she had always done before. She opened her mouth to speak and doubled over, clutching at her stomach as though an animal were devouring her. Sweat beaded her forehead and she planted her feet wide apart on the ground as if this animal would be born. Though her vision was barred with pain, she saw Harriet's tearfilled eyes, searching hers.

'Let's not go back to the apartment,' Sadie said, hearing her own words as if they issued not from her mouth but from a pit in the ground. 'Let's not go back there . . . let's you and me go out in the world . . . just the two of us.' A second before covering her face to hide her shame Sadie glimpsed Harriet's eyes, impossibly close to her own, their pupils pointed with a hatred such as she had never seen before.

It seemed to Sadie that it was taking an eternity for

her sister to leave. 'Go away . . . go away . . . or I'll suffocate.' She was moaning the words over and over again, her face buried deep in her hands. 'Go away . . . please go away . . . I'll suffocate. . . .' She could not tell, however, whether she was thinking these words or speaking them aloud.

At last she heard Harriet's footstep on the dry branches, as she started out of the clearing. Sadie listened, but although one step followed another, the cracking sound of the dry branches did not grow any fainter as Harriet penetrated farther into the grove. Sadie knew then that this agony she was suffering was itself the dreaded voyage into the world—the very voyage she had always feared Harriet would make. That she herself was making it instead of Harriet did not affect her certainty that this was it.

Sadie stood at the souvenir booth looking at some birchbark canoes. The wind was blowing colder and stronger than it had a while ago, or perhaps it only seemed this way to her, so recently returned from the airless clearing. She did not recall her trip back through the grove; she was conscious only of her haste to buy some souvenirs and to leave. Some chains of paper tacked to the side of the booth as decoration kept flying into her face. The Indian chief was smiling at her from behind the counter of souvenirs.

'What can I do for you?' he asked.

'I'm leaving,' said Sadie, 'so I want souvenirs. . . .'

'Take your choice; you've got birchbark canoes with or without mailing cards attached, Mexican sombrero ashtrays, exhilarating therapeutic pine cushions filled with the regional needles . . . and banners for a boy's room.'

'There's no boy home,' Sadie said, having caught only these last words.

'How about cushions . . . or canoes?'

She nodded.

'Which do you want?'

'Both,' she answered quickly.

'How many?'

Sadie closed her eyes. Try as she would she could not count up the members of the family. She could not even reach an approximate figure. 'Eleven,' she blurted out finally, in desperation.

'Eleven of each?' he asked raising his eyebrows.

'Yes . . . yes,' she answered quickly, batting the paper chains out of her face, 'eleven of each.'

'You sure don't forget the old folks at home, do you?' he said, beginning to collect the canoes. He made an individual package of each souvenir and then wrapped them all together in coarse brown paper which he bound with thick twine.

Sadie had given him a note and he was punching his money belt for the correct change when her eyes fell on his light, freckled hand. Startled, she shifted her glance from his hand punching the nickel belt to his brick-coloured face streaked with purple and vermilion paint. For the first time she noticed his Irish blue eyes. Slowly the hot flush of shame crept along the nape of her neck. It was the same unbearable mortification that she had experienced in the clearing; it spread upward from her neck to the roots of her hair, colouring her face a dark red. That she was ashamed for the Indian this time and not of her own words, failed to lessen the intensity of her suffering; the boundaries of her pride had never been firmly fixed inside herself. She stared intently at his Irish blue eyes, so oddly light in his brick-coloured face. What was it? She was tormented by the sight of an incongruity she couldn't name. All at once she remembered the pavilion and the people dining there; her heart started to pound. 'They'll see it,' she said to herself in a panic. 'They'll see it and they'll know that I've seen it too.' Somehow this latter possibility was the most perilous of all.

'They must never know I've seen it,' she said, grinding her teeth, and she leaned over the counter, crushing some canoes under her chest. 'Quickly,' she whispered. 'Go out your little door and meet me back of the booth. . . .'

A second later she found him there. 'Listen!' She clutched his hand. 'We must hurry . . . I didn't mean to see you . . . I'm sorry . . . I've been trying not to look at you for years . . . for years and years and years. . . .' She gaped at him in horror. 'Why are you standing there? We've got to hurry. . . . They haven't caught me looking at you yet, but we've got to hurry.' She headed for the bridge, leading the Indian behind her. He followed quickly without saying a word.

The water's roar increased in volume as they approached the opposite bank of the chasm, and Sadie found relief in the sound. Once off the bridge she ran as fast as she could along the path leading to the waterfall. The Indian followed close on her heels, his hand resting lightly in her own, as Harriet's had earlier when they'd sped together through the grove. Reaching the waterfall, she edged along the wall of rock until she stood directly behind the water's cascade. With a cry of delight she leaned back in the curve of the wall, insensible to its icy dampness, which penetrated even through the thickness of her woollen coat. She listened to the cataract's deafening roar and her heart almost burst for joy, because she had hidden the Indian safely behind the cascade where he could be neither seen nor heard. She turned around and smiled at him kindly. He too smiled, and she no longer saw in his face any trace of the incongruity that had shocked her so before.

The foaming waters were beautiful to see. Sadie stepped forward, holding her hand out to the Indian.

When Harriet awakened that morning all traces of her earlier victorious mood had vanished. She felt certain that disaster would overtake her before she could start out for Pocahontas Falls. Heavyhearted and with fumbling hands, she set about making her pack. Luncheon with Sadie was an impossible cliff which she did not have the necessary strength to scale. When she came to three round cushions that had to be snapped into their rainproof casings she gave up with a groan and rushed headlong out of her cabin in search of Beryl.

Fortunately Beryl waited table on the second shift and so she found her reading a magazine with one leg flung over the arm of her chair.

'I can't make my pack,' Harriet said hysterically, bursting into Beryl's cabin without even knocking at the door.

Beryl swung her leg around and got out of her chair, 'I'll make your pack,' she said in a calm voice, knocking some tobacco out of her pipe. 'I would have come around this morning, but you said last night you wanted to make it alone.'

'It's Sadie,' Harriet complained. 'It's that cursed lunch with Sadie. I can't go through with it. I know I can't. I shouldn't have to in the first place. She's not even supposed to be here. . . . I'm an ass. . . .'

'To hell with sisters,' said Beryl. 'Give 'em all a good swift kick in the pants.'

'She's going to stop me from going on my canoe trip . . . I know she is. . . .' Harriet had adopted the whining tone of a little girl.

'No, she isn't,' said Beryl, speaking with authority.

'Why not?' Harriet asked. She looked at Beryl almost wistfully.

'She'd better not try anything . . .' said Beryl. 'Ever hear of ju-jitsu?' She grunted with satisfaction. 'Come on, we'll go make your pack.' She was so pleased with Harriet's new state of dependency that she was rapidly overcoming her original shyness. An hour later she had completed the pack, and Harriet was dressed and ready.

'Will you go with me to the souvenir booth?' she begged the waitress. 'I don't want to meet her alone.' She was in a worse state of nerves than ever.

'I'll go with you,' said Beryl, 'but let's stop at my cabin on the way so I can change into my uniform. I'm on duty soon.'

They were nearly twenty minutes late arriving at the booth, and Harriet was therefore rather surprised not to see Sadie standing there. 'Perhaps she's been here and gone back to the lodge for a minute,' she said to Beryl. 'I'll find out.' She walked up to the souvenir counter and questioned the Indian, with whom she was slightly familiar. 'Was there a woman waiting her a while ago, Timothy?' she asked.

'A dark middle-aged woman?'

'That's right.'

'She was here for an hour or more,' he said, 'never budged from this stall until about fifteen minutes ago.'

'She couldn't have been here an hour!' Harriet argued. 'Not my sister. . . . I told her one-thirty and it's not yet two.'

'Then it wasn't your sister. The woman who was

here stayed more than an hour, without moving. I noticed her because it was such a queer-looking thing. I noticed her first from my chair at the bridge and then when I came up here she was still standing by the booth. She must have stood here over an hour.'

'Then it was a different middle-aged woman.'

'That may be,' he agreed, 'but anyway, this one left about fifteen minutes ago. After standing all that time she turned around all of a sudden and bought a whole bunch of souvenirs from me . . . then just when I was punching my belt for the change she said something I couldn't understand—it sounded like Polish—and then she lit out for the bridge before I could give her a penny. That woman's got impulses,' he added with a broad grin. 'If she's your sister, I'll give you her change, in case she don't stop here on her way back. . . . But she sounded to me like a Polak.'

'Beryl,' said Harriet, 'run across the bridge and see if Sadie's behind the waterfall. I'm sure this Polish woman wasn't Sadie, but they might both be back there. . . . If she's not there, we'll look in the lodge.'

When Beryl returned her face was dead white; she stared at Harriet in silence, and even when Harriet finally grabbed hold of her shoulders and shook her hard, she would not say anything.

A DAY IN THE OPEN

In the outskirts of the capital there was a low white house, very much like the other houses around it. The street on which it stood was not paved, as this was a poor section of the city. The door of this particular house, very new and studded with nails, was bolted inside and out. A large room, furnished with some modern chromium chairs, a bar, and an electric record machine, opened onto the empty *patio*. A fat little Indian boy was seated in one of the chairs, listening to the tune *Good Night, Sweetheart*, which he had just chosen. It was playing at full volume and the little boy was staring very seriously ahead of him at the machine. This was one of the houses owned and run by Señor Kurten, who was half Spanish and half German.

It was a grey afternoon. In one of the bedrooms Julia and Inez had just awakened. Julia was small and monkey-like. She was appealing only because of her extraordinarily large and luminous eyes. Inez was tall and high-breasted. Her head was a bit too small for her body and her eyes were too close together. She wore her hair in stiff waves.

Julia was moaning on her bed.

'My stomach is worse today,' she said to Inez. 'Come over and feel it. The lump on the right side is bigger.' She twisted her head on the pillow and sighed. Inez was staring sternly into space.

'No,' she said to Julia. 'I cannot bear to feel that lump. *Santa Maria!* With something like that inside me I should go wild.' She made a wry face and shuddered.

'You must not feel it if you do not want to,' said Julia drowsily. Inez poured herself some *guaro*. She was a heavy drinker but her vitality remained unimpaired, although her skin often broke out in pimples. She ate violet lozenges to cover the smell of liquor on her breath and often popped six or seven of them into her mouth at once. Being full of enterprise she often made more money outside the whorehouse than she did at her regular job.

Julia was Mexican and a great favourite with the men, who enjoyed feeling that they were endangering her very life by going to bed with her.

'Well,' said Inez, 'I think that this afternoon I will go

to the movies, if you will lend me a pair of your stockings. You had better lie here in your bed. I would sit here with you but it makes me feel very strange now to stay in this room. It is peculiar because, you know, I am a very calm woman and have suffered a great deal since I was born. You should go to a doctor,' she added.

'I cannot bear to be out in the street,' said Julia. 'The sun is too hot and the wind is too cold. The smell of the market makes me feel sick, although I have known it all my life. No sooner have I walked a few blocks than I must find some park to sit in, I am so tired. Then somebody comes and tries to sell me orchids and I buy them. I have been out three times this week and each time I have bought some flowers. Now you know I can't afford to do this, but I am so weak and ill that I am becoming more like my grandmother every day. She had a feeling that she was not wanted here on this earth, either by God or by other people, so she never felt that she could refuse anyone anything.'

'Well, if you are going to become like your grandmother,' said Inez, 'it will be a sad mistake. I should forget this sort of thing. You'll get to the doctor. Meanwhile, sit in the sun more. I don't want to be unkind. . . .'

'No, no. You are not unkind,' Julia protested.

'You sit in this dark room all day long even when there is sun and you do not feel so sick.'

Julia was feeling more desperately lonely than she had ever felt before in her life. She patted her heart. Suddenly the door pushed open and Señor Kurten came into the room. He was a slight man with a low forehead and a long nose.

'Julia and Inez,' he said. 'Señor Ramirez just telephoned that he is coming over this afternoon with a friend. He is going to take you both out to the country on a picnic and you are to hurry up and be ready. Try to bring them back to the bar in the evening.'

'Hans,' said Julia. 'I am sick. I can't see Señor Ramirez or anyone else.'

'Well, you know I can't do anything if he wants to see you. If he was angry he could make too much trouble. I am sorry.' Señor Kurten left the room, closing the door slowly behind him.

'He is so important,' said Inez, rubbing some eau de cologne over Julia's forehead. 'So important, poor child. You must go.' Her hand was hard and dry.

'Inez—' Julia clutched at Inez's *kimono* just as she was walking away. She struggled out of bed and threw herself into the arms of her friend. Inez was obliged to brace herself against the foot of the bed to keep from being knocked over.

'Don't make yourself crazy,' said Inez to Julia, but then Inez began to cry; the sound was high like the squeal of a pig.

'Inez,' said Julia. 'Get dressed and don't cry. I feel better, my little baby.'

They went into the bar and sat down to await the arrival of Señor Ramirez and his friend. Julia's arm was flung over the side of the chair, and her purse was swinging from her hand on an unusually long strap. She had put a little red dot in the corner of each eye, and rouged her cheeks very highly.

'You don't look very good,' said Inez. 'I'm afraid in my heart for you.'

Julia opened her eyes wide and stared fixedly ahead of her at the wall. The Indian boy was polishing a very large alarm clock with care.

Soon Señor Ramirez stuck his head through the doorway. He had a German face but there was something very Spanish in the angle of his slouched *fedora* hat. His moustaches were blond and abundant. He had just shaved, and the talcum powder was visible on his chin and on his cheeks. He wore a pink shirt and a light tweed jacket, and on the fourth finger of each hand a heavy gold ring studded with a jewel.

'Come on, daughters,' he said. 'The car is waiting outside, with my friend. Move along.'

Señor Ramirez drove very quickly. Julia and Inez sat uncomfortably on the edge of the back seat, hanging onto the straps at the side.

'We are going on a picnic,' shouted Señor Ramirez. 'I've brought with me five bottles of champagne. They are in the back of the car and they were all packed in ice by my cook. There is no reason why we should not have everything we want with us. They are inside a basket in the back. She wrapped the ice in a towel. That way it doesn't melt so quickly, but still we have to get there in a pretty short time. I drink nothing but American whisky, so I brought along a quart of it for myself. What do you think of that?'

'Oh, how nice,' said Julia.

'I think we shall have a wonderful time,' said Inez.

Señor Ramirez's friend Alfredo looked ill and disgruntled. He did not say anything himself, nor did the angle of his head indicate that he was listening to a word that anyone else was saying.

It was a cold day and the parasols under which the policemen stood were flapping in the wind. They passed a new yellow brick building, high at the top of six or seven flights of yellow brick steps.

'That is going to be a new museum,' said Señor Ramirez. 'When it opens we are all going to have a big dinner there together. Everyone there will be an old friend of mine. That's nothing. I can have dinner with fifty people every night of my life.'

'A life of *fiesta*,' put in Inez.

'Even more than that. They are more than just *fiestas*,' he said, without quite knowing what he meant himself.

The sun was shining into Julia's lap. She felt light-headed and feverish. Señor Ramirez turned the radio on as loud as he could. They were broadcasting *Madame Butterfly* as the car reached the outskirts of the city.

'I have three radios at home,' said Señor Ramirez.

'Ah,' said Inez. 'One for the morning, one for the night and one for the afternoon.' Julia listened to Inez with interest and wonder. They were on the edge of a deep ravine, going round a curve in the road. The mountainside across the ravine was in the shade, and some Indians were climbing toward the summit.

'Walk, walk, walk . . .' said Julia mournfully. 'Oh, how tired it makes me feel to watch them.'

Inez pinched her friend's arm. 'Listen,' she whispered to her. 'You are not in your room. You daren't say things like that. You must not speak of being tired. It's no fun for them. They wouldn't like it.'

'We'll be coming to that picnic spot in a minute,' said Señor Ramirez. 'Nobody knows where it is but me. I like to have a spot, you know, where all my friends won't come and disturb me. Alfredo,' he added, 'are you hungry?'

'I don't think this Alfredo is very nice, do you?' Inez asked very softly of Julia.

'Oh, yes,' said Julia, for she was not quick to detect a mean nature in anybody, being altogether kind and charitable herself. At last, after driving through a path wide enough for only one car, they arrived at the picnic spot. It was a fair-sized clearing in a little forest. Not far from it, at the bottom of a hill, was a little river and a waterfall. They got out and listened to the noise of the water. Both of the women were delighted with the sound.

'Since it is so sunny out, ladies,' said Señor Ramirez, 'I am going to walk around in my underpants. I hope that my friend will do the same if he wants to.'

'What a lucky thing for us,' said Inez in a strident voice. 'The day begins right.' Señor Ramirez undressed and slipped on a pair of tennis shoes. His legs were very white and freckled.

'Now I will give you some champagne right away,' he said to them, a little out of breath because he had struggled so quickly out of his clothes. He went over to where he had laid the basket and took from it a champagne bottle. On his way back he stumbled over a rock; the bottle fell from his hand and was smashed in many pieces. For a moment his face clouded over and he looked as though he were about to lose his temper; instead, seizing another bottle from the basket, he flung it high into the air, almost over the tops of the trees. He returned elated to his friends.

'A gentleman,' he said, 'always knows how to make fun. I am one of the richest businessmen in this country. I am also the craziest. Like an American. When I am out I always have a wonderful time, and so does everyone who is with me, because they know that while I am around there is always plenty. Plenty to eat, plenty to drink, and plenty of beautiful women to make love to. Once you have been out with me,' he pointed his finger at Julia and Inez, 'any other man will seem to you like an old-lady schoolteacher.'

He turned to Alfredo. 'Tell me, my friend, have you not had the time of your life with me?'

'Yes, I have,' said Alfredo. He was thinking very noticeably of other things.

'His mind is always on business,' Señor Ramirez explained to Julia. 'He is also very clever. I have gotten him this job with a German concern. They are manufacturing planes.' Alfredo said something to Señor Ramirez in German, and they spoke no longer on the subject. They spread out their picnic lunch and sat down to eat.

Señor Ramirez insisted on feeding Julia with his own fingers. This rather vexed Inez, so she devoted herself to eating copiously. Señor Ramirez drank quantities of whisky out of a tin folding cup. At the end of fifteen or twenty minutes he was already quite drunk.

'Now, isn't it wonderful to be all together like this, friends? Alfredo, aren't these two women the finest, sweetest women in the world? I do not understand why in the eyes of God they should be condemned to the fires of Hell for what they are. Do you?'

Julia moaned and rose to her feet.

'No, no!' she said, looking up helplessly at the branches overhead.

'Come on,' said Señor Ramirez. 'We're not going to worry about this today, are we?' He took hold of her wrist and pulled her down to the ground beside him. Julia hid her face in her hands and leaned her head against his shoulder. Soon she was smiling up at him and stroking his face.

'You won't leave me alone?' she asked, laughing a little in an effort to bring him to terms with her. If anyone were to be pitted successfully against the Divine, she thought, it would certainly be someone like Señor Ramirez. The presence of such men is often enough to dispel fear from the hearts of certain people for whom God is more of an enemy than a friend. Señor Ramirez's principal struggle in life was one of pride rather than of conscience; and because his successes were numerous each day, replenishing his energy and his taste for life, his strength was easily felt by those around him. Now that he was near her, Julia felt that she was safe from Hell, and she was quite happy even though her side still hurt her very badly.

'Now,' said Inez, 'I think that we should all play a game, to chase gloomy thoughts out of this girl's head.'

She rose to her feet and snatched Señor Ramirez's hat from where it lay beside him on the ground, placing it a few feet away upside down on the grass. Then she gathered some acorns in the picnic basket.

'Now,' she said. 'We will see who can throw these acorns into the hat. He will win.'

'I think,' said Señor Ramirez, 'that the two women should be naked while we are playing this; otherwise it will be just a foolish children's game.'

'And we are not children at all,' said Inez, winking

at him. The two women turned and looked at Alfredo questioningly.

'Oh, don't mind him,' said Señor Ramirez. 'He sees nothing but numbers in his head.'

The two girls went behind some bushes and undressed. When they returned, Alfredo was bending over a ledger and trying to explain something to Señor Ramirez, who looked up, delighted that they had returned so quickly, so that he would not be obliged to listen.

'Ah,' he said. 'Now this looks much more like friends together, doesn't it, Alfredo?'

'Come on,' said Inez. 'We will all get into line here with this basket and each one will try to throw the acorn into the hat.'

Señor Ramirez grew quite excited playing the game; then he began to get angry because he never managed to get the acorn into the hat. Inez screeched with laughter and threw her acorn wider and wider of the mark, each time purposely, in order to soothe, if possible, the hurt pride of Señor Ramirez. Alfredo refused to play at all.

'Games don't interest me,' said Señor Ramirez suddenly. 'I'd like to play longer with you, daughters, but I can't honestly keep my mind on the game.'

'It is of no importance at all, really,' said Inez, busily trying to think up something to do next.

'How are your wife and children?' Julia asked him.

Inez bit her lip and shook her head.

'They are well taken care of. I have sent them to a little town where they are staying in a pension. Quiet women—all three of them—the little girls and the mother. I am going to sleep.' He stretched out under a tree and put his hat over his face. Alfredo was absorbed in his ledger. Inez and Julia sat side by side and waited.

'You have the brain of a baby chicken,' Inez said to Julia. 'I must think for both of us. If I had not had a great deal of practice when I had to keep count of all the hundreds of *tortillas* that I sold for my mother, I don't know where we would be.'

'Dead, probably,' said Julia. They began to feel cold.

'Come,' said Inez. 'Sing with me.' They sang a song about leaving and never returning, four or five times through. When Señor Ramirez awakened he suggested to Julia that they go for a walk. She accepted sweetly, and so they started off through the woods. Soon they reached a good-sized field where Señor Ramirez suggested that they sit for a while.

'The first time I went to bed with a woman,' he said, 'it was in the country like this. The land belonged to my father. Three or four times a day we would come out into the fields and make love. She loved it, and would have come more often if I had asked her to. Some years later I went to her wedding and I had a terrible fight there. I don't even remember who the man was, but in the end he was badly hurt. I can tell you that.'

'If you put your arms around me,' said Julia, 'I will feel less cold. You don't mind my asking you to do this, but I love you very much and I feel very contented with you.'

'That's good,' said Señor Ramirez, looking off at the mountains and shielding his eyes from the sun. He was listening to the sound of the waterfall, which was louder here. Julia was laughing and touching various parts of his body.

'Ah,' she said. 'I don't mind my side hurting me so badly if I can only be happy the way I am now with you. You are so sweet and so wonderful.'

He gave her a quick loud kiss on the mouth and rose to his feet.

'Listen,' he said. 'Wouldn't you like to come into the water with me?'

'I am too sick a woman to go into the water, and I am a little bit afraid.'

'In my arms you don't have to be afraid. I will carry you. The current would be too strong for you to manage anyway.' Señor Ramirez was now as gay as a lark, although he had been bored but a moment before. He liked nothing better than performing little feats that were assured of success from the beginning. He carried her down to the river, singing at the top of his voice.

The noise of the falls was very loud here, and Julia clung tightly to her escort.

'Don't let go, now,' she said. But her voice seemed

to fly away behind her like a ribbon caught in the wind. They were in the water and Señor Ramirez began to walk in the direction of the falls.

'I will hold tight, all right,' he said. 'Because the water runs pretty swiftly near the falls.' He seemed to enjoy stepping precariously from one stone to another with Julia in his arms.

'This is not so easy, you know. This is damned hard. The stones are slippery.' Julia tightened her grip around his neck and kissed him quickly all over his face.

'If I let you go,' he said, 'the current would carry you along like a leaf over the falls, and then one of those big rocks would make a hole in your head. That would be the end, of course.' Julia's eyes widened with horror, and she yelled with the suddenness of an animal just wounded.

'But why do you scream like that, Julia? I love you, sweetheart.' He had had enough of struggling through the water, and so he turned around and started back.

'Are we going away from the waterfall?'

'Yes. It was wonderful, wasn't it?'

'Very nice,' she said.

He grew increasingly careless as the current slackened, with the result that he miscalculated and his foot slipped between two stones. This threw him off his balance and he fell. He was unhurt, but the back of Julia's head had hit a stone. It started to bleed profusely. He struggled to his feet and carried her to the riverbank. She was not sure that she was not dying, and hugged him all the more closely. Pulling her along, he walked quickly up the hill and back through the woods to where Inez and Alfredo were still sitting.

'It will be all right, won't it?' she asked him a bit weakly.

'Those damn rocks were slippery,' he growled. He was sulky, and eager to be on his way home.

'Oh, God of mine!' lamented Inez, when she saw what had happened. 'What a sad ending for a walk! Terrible things always happen to Julia. She is a daughter of misfortune. It's a lucky thing that I am just the contrary.'

Señor Ramirez was in such a hurry to leave the picnic spot that he did not even want to bother to collect the various baskets and plates he had brought with him. They dressed, and he yelled for them all to get into the car. Julia wrapped a shawl around her bleeding head. Inez went around snatching up all the things, like an enraged person.

'Can I have these things?' she asked her host. He nodded his head impatiently. Julia was by now crying rhythmically like a baby that has almost fallen asleep.

The two women sat huddled together in the back of the car. Inez explained to Julia that she was going to make presents of the plates and baskets to her family. She shed a tear or two herself. When they arrived at the house, Señor Ramirez handed some banknotes to Inez from where he was sitting.

'*Adios*,' he said. The two women got out of the car and stood in the street.

'Will you come back again?' Julia asked him tenderly, ceasing to cry for a moment.

'Yes. I'm coming back again,' he said. '*Adios*.' He pressed his foot on the accelerator and drove off.

The bar was packed with men. Inez led Julia around through the *patio* to their room. When she had shut the door, she slipped the banknotes into her pocket and put the baskets on the floor.

'Do you want any of these baskets?' she asked.

Julia was sitting on the edge of her bed, looking into space. 'No, thank you,' she said. Inez looked at her, and saw that she was far away.

'Señor Ramirez gave me four drinking cups made out of plastic,' said Inez. 'Do you want one of them for yourself?'

Julia did not answer right away. Then she said: 'Will he come back?'

'I don't know,' Inez said. 'I'm going to the movies. I'll come and see you afterwards, before I go into the bar.'

'All right,' said Julia. But Inez knew that she did not care. She shrugged her shoulders and went out through the door, closing it behind her.

A QUARRELLING PAIR

The two puppets are sisters in their early fifties. The puppet stage should have a rod or string dividing it down the middle to indicate two rooms. One puppet is seated on each side of the dividing line. If it is not possible to seat them they will have to stand. Mildred, the older puppet, is stronger-looking and wears brighter colours.

Mildred (the stronger puppet): I hope you are beginning to think about our milk.

Rhoda (after a pause): Well, I'm not.

Mildred: Now what's the matter with you? You're

not going to have a visitation from our dead, are you?

Rhoda: I don't have visitations this winter because I'm too tired to love even our dead. Anyway, I'm disgusted with the world.

Mildred: Just mind your business. I mind mine and I *am* thinking about our milk.

Rhoda: I'm so tired of being sad. I'd like to change.

Mildred: You don't get enough enjoyment out of your room. Why don't you?

Rhoda: Oh, because the world and its sufferers are always on my mind.

Mildred: That's not normal. You're not smart enough to be of any use to the outside, anyway.

Rhoda: If I were young I'd succour the sick. I wouldn't care about culture, even, if I were young.

Mildred: You don't have any knack for making a home. There's blessed satisfaction in that, at any rate.

Rhoda: My heart's too big to make a home.

Mildred: No. It's because you have no self-sufficiency. If I wasn't around, you wouldn't have the leisure to worry. You're a lost soul, when I'm not around. You don't even have the pep to worry about the outside when I'm not around. Not that the outside loses by that! *(She sniffs with scorn.)*

Rhoda: You're right. But I swear that my heart is big.

Mildred: I've come to believe that what is inside of people is not so very interesting. You can breed considerable discontent around you with a big heart, and considerable harmony with a small one. Compare your living-quarters to mine. And my heart is small like Papa's was.

Rhoda: You chill me to the marrow when you tell me that your heart is small. You do love me, though, don't you?

Mildred: You're my sister, aren't you?

Rhoda: Sisterly love is one of the few boons in this life.

Mildred: Now, that's enough exaggerating. I could enumerate other things.

Rhoda: I suppose it's wicked to squeeze love from a

small heart. I suppose it's a sin. I suppose God meant for small hearts to be busy with other things.

Mildred: Possibly. Let's have our milk in my room. It's so much more agreeable to sit in here. Partly because I'm a neater woman than you are.

Rhoda: Even though you have a small heart, I wish there were no one but you and me in the world. Then I would never feel that I had to go among the others.

Mildred: Well, I wish I could hand you my gift for contentment in a box. It would be so lovely if you were like me. Then we could have our milk in *either* room. One day in your room and the next day in mine.

Rhoda: I'm sure that's the sort of thing that never happens.

Mildred: It happens in a million homes, seven days a week. I'm the type that's in the majority.

Rhoda: Never, never, never . . . .

Mildred (very firmly): It happens in a million homes.

Rhoda: Never, never, never!

Mildred (rising): Are you going to listen to me when

I tell you that it happens in a million homes, or must I lose my temper?

Rhoda: You have already lost it. *(Mildred exits rapidly in a rage. Rhoda goes to the chimes and sings:)*

My horse was frozen like a stone
A long, long time ago.
Frozen near the flower bed
In the wintry sun.
Or maybe in the night time
Or maybe not at all.

My horse runs across the fields
On many afternoons.
Black as dirt and filled with blood
I glimpse him fleeing toward the woods
And then not at all.

Mildred (offstage): I'm coming with your milk, and I hope the excitement is over for today. *(Enters carrying two small white glasses.)* Oh, why do I bring milk to a person who is dead-set on making my life a real hell?

Rhoda (clasping her hands with feeling): Yes. Why? Why? Why? Why? Oh, what a hideous riddle!

Mildred: You love to pretend that everything is a riddle. You think that's the way to be intellectual. There is no riddle. I am simply keeping up my end of the bargain.

Rhoda: Oh, bargains, bargains, bargains!

Mildred: Will you let me finish, you excitable thing? I'm trying to explain that I'm behaving the way I was moulded to behave. I happen to be appreciative of the mould I was cast in, and neither heaven nor earth is going to make me damage it. Your high-strung emotions are not going to affect me. Here's your milk. *(She enters Rhoda's side of the stage and hands her the milk, but Rhoda punches the bottom of the glass with her closed fist and sends it flying out of Mildred's hand. Mildred deals Rhoda a terrific blow on the face and scurries back to her own room. There is silence for a moment. Then Mildred buries her face in her hands and weeps. Rhoda exits and Mildred goes to the chimes and sings:)*

Mildred (singing):

> I dreamed I climbed upon a cliff,
> My sister's hand in mine.
> Then searched the valley for my house
> But only sunny fields could see
> And the church spire shining.
> I searched until my heart was cold
> But only sunny fields could see
> And the church spire shining.

A girl ran down the mountainside
With bluebells in her hat.
I asked the valley for her name
But only wind and rain could hear
And the church bell tolling.
I asked until my lips were cold
But wakened not yet knowing
If the name she bore was my sister's name
Or if it was my own.

(Rhoda enters her side of the stage.)

Mildred: Rhoda?

Rhoda: What do you want?

Mildred: Go away if you like.

Rhoda: The moment hasn't come yet, and it won't come today because the day is finished and the evening is here. Thank God!

Mildred: I know I should get some terrible disease and die if I thought I did not live in the right. It would break my heart.

Rhoda: You do live in the right, sweetie, so don't think about it. *(Pause.)* I'll go and get your milk.

Mildred: I'll go too. But let's drink it in here because it really *is* much pleasanter in here, isn't it? *(They rise.)* Oh, I'm so glad the evening has come! I'm nervously exhausted. *(They exit.)*

A STICK OF GREEN CANDY

The clay pit had been dug in the side of a long hill. By leaning back against the lower part of its wall, Mary could see the curved highway above her and the cars speeding past. On the other side of the highway the hill continued rising, but at a steeper angle. If she tilted her head farther back, she could glimpse the square house on the hill's summit, with its flight of stone steps that led from the front door down to the kerb, dividing the steep lawn in two.

She had been playing in the pit for a long time. Like many other children, she fancied herself at the head of a regiment; at the same time, she did not join in any neighbourhood games, preferring to play all alone in the pit, which lay about a mile beyond the edge of town. She was a scrupulously clean child with a strong, immobile face and long, well-arranged curls. Sometimes when she went home toward evening there were traces of clay on her dark coat, even though she had worked diligently with the brush she carried along every afternoon. She despised untidiness, and she feared that the clay might betray her headquarters, which she suspected the other children of planning to invade.

One afternoon she stumbled and fell on the clay when it was still slippery and wet from a recent rainfall. She never failed to leave the pit before twilight, but this time she decided to wait until it was dark so that her sullied coat would attract less attention. Wisely she refrained from using her brush on the wet clay.

Having always left the pit at an earlier hour, she felt that an explanation was due to her soldiers; to announce simply that she had fallen down was out of the question. She knew that her men trusted her and would therefore accept in good faith any reason she chose to give them for this abrupt change in her day's routine, but convincing herself was a more difficult task. She never told them anything until she really believed what she was going to say. After concentrating a few minutes, she summoned them with a bugle call.

'Men,' she began, once they were lined up at attention, 'I'm staying an hour longer today than usual, so I can work on the mountain goat manœuvres. I explained mountain goat fighting last week, but I'll tell you what it is again. It's a special technique used in the mountains around big cliffs. No machine can do mountain goat fighting. We're going to specialize.' She paused. 'Even though I'm staying, I want you to go right ahead and have your recreation hour as usual, like you always do the minute I leave. I have total respect for your recreation, and I know you fight as hard as you play.'

She dismissed them and walked up to her own headquarters in the deepest part of the pit. At the end of the day the colour of the red pit deepened; then, after the sun had sunk behind the hill, the clay lost its colour. She began to feel cold and a little uneasy. She was so accustomed to leaving her men each day at the same hour, just before they thronged into the gymnasium, that now lingering on made her feel like an intruder.

It was almost night when she climbed out of the pit. She glanced up at the hilltop house and then started down toward the deserted lower road. When she reached the outskirts of town she chose the darkest streets so that her coat would be less noticeable. She hated the thick pats of clay that were embedded in its wool; moreover she was suffering from a sense of inner untidiness as a result of the unexpected change in her daily routine. She walked along slowly, scuffing her heels, her face wearing the expression of a person surfeited with food. Far underneath her increasingly lethargic mood lurked a feeling of apprehension; she knew she would be reprimanded for returning home after dark, but she never would admit either the possibility of punishment or the fear of it. At this period she was rapidly perfecting a psychological mechanism which enabled her to forget, for long stretches of time, that her parents existed.

She found her father in the vestibule hanging his coat up on a peg. Her heart sank as he turned around to greet her. Without seeming to, he took in the pats of clay at a glance, but his shifting eyes never alighted candidly on any object.

'You've been playing in that pit below the Speed house again,' he said to her. 'From now on, I want you to play at the Kinsey Memorial Grounds.' Since he appeared to have nothing further to say, she started away, but immediately he continued. 'Some day you may have to live in a town where the administration doesn't make any provision for children at all. Or it may provide you with a small plot of land and a couple of dinky swings. There's a very decent sum goes each year to the Grounds here. They provide you with swings, seesaws and chin bars.' He glanced furtively at her coat. 'Tomorrow,' he said, 'I drive past that pit on my way out to Sam's. I'll draw up to the edge of the road and look down. See that you're over at the Memorial Grounds with the other children.'

Mary never passed the playgrounds without quickening her step. This site, where the screams of several dozen children mingled with the high, grinding sound of the moving swings, she had always automatically hated. It was the antithesis of her clay pit and the well-ordered barracks inside it.

When she went to bed, she was in such a state of wild excitement that she was unable to sleep. It was the first time that her father's observations had not made her feel either humiliated or ill. The following day after school she set out for the pit. As she was climbing the long hill (she always approached her barracks from the lower road), she slackened her pace and stood still. All at once she had had the fear that by looking into her eyes the soldiers might divine her father's existence. To each one of them she was like himself—a man without a family. After a minute she resumed her climb. When she reached the edge of the pit, she put both feet together and jumped inside.

'Men,' she said, once she had blown the bugle and made a few routine announcements, 'I know you have hard muscles in your legs. But how would you like to have even harder ones?' It was a rhetorical question to which she did not expect an answer. 'We're going to have hurdle races and plain running every day now for two hours.'

Though in her mind she knew dimly that this intensified track training was preparatory to an imminent battle on the Memorial playgrounds, she did not dare discuss it with her men, or even think about it too precisely herself. She had to avoid coming face to face with an impossibility.

'As we all know,' she continued, 'we don't like to have teams because we've been through too much on the battlefield all together. Every day I'll divide you up fresh before the racing, so that the ones who are against each other today, for instance, will be running on the same side tomorrow. The men in our outfit are funny about taking sides against each other, even just in play and athletics. The other outfits in this country don't feel the same as we do.'

She dug her hands into her pockets and hung her head sheepishly. She was fine now, and certain of victory. She could feel the men's hearts bursting with love for her and with pride in their regiment. She looked up—a car was rounding the bend, and as it came nearer she recognized it as her father's.

'Men,' she said in a clear voice, 'you can do what you want for thirty minutes while I make out the racing schedule and the team lists.' She stared unflinchingly at the dark blue sedan and waited with perfect outward calm for her father to slow down; she was still waiting after the car had curved out of sight. When she realized that he was gone, she held her breath. She expected her heart to leap for joy, but it did not.

'Now I'll go to my headquarters,' she announced in a flat voice. 'I'll be back with the team lists in twenty-five minutes.' She glanced up at the highway; she felt oddly disappointed and uneasy. A small figure was descending the stone steps on the other side of the highway. It was a boy. She watched in amazement; she had never seen anyone come down these steps before. Since the highway had replaced the old country road, the family living in the hilltop house came and went through the back door.

Watching the boy, she felt increasingly certain that he was on his way down to the pit. He stepped off the kerb after looking prudently for cars in each direction; then he crossed the highway and clambered down the hill. Just as she had expected him to, when he reached the edge of the pit he seated himself on the ground and slid into it, smearing his coat—dark like her own—with clay.

'It's a big clay pit,' he said, looking up at her. He was younger than she, but he looked straight into her eyes without a trace of shyness. She knew he was a stranger in town; she had never seen him before. This made him less detestable, nonetheless she had to be rid of him shortly because the men were expecting her back with the team lists.

'Where do you come from?' she asked him.

'From inside that house.' He pointed at the hilltop.

'Where do you live when you're not visiting?'

'I live inside that house,' he repeated, and he sat down on the floor of the pit.

'Sit on the orange crate,' she ordered him severely. 'You don't pay any attention to your coat.'

He shook his head. She was exasperated with him because he was untidy, and he had lied to her. She knew perfectly well that he was merely a visitor in the hilltop house.

'Why did you come out this door?' she asked, looking at him sharply. 'The people in that house go out the back. It's level there and they've got a drive.'

'I don't know why,' he answered simply.

'Where do you come from?' she asked again.

'That's my house.' He pointed to it as if she were asking him for the first time. 'The driveway in back's got gravel in it. I've got a whole box of it in my room. I can bring it down.'

'No gravel's coming in here that belongs to a liar,' she interrupted him. 'Tell me where you come from and then you can go get it.'

He stood up. 'I live in that big house up there,' he said calmly. 'From my room I can see the river, the road down there and the road up here, and this pit and you.'

'It's not your room!' she shouted angrily. 'You're a visitor there. I was a visitor last year at my aunt's.'

'Good-bye.'

He was climbing out of the pit. Once outside he turned around and looked down at her. There was an expression of fulfilment on his face.

'I'll bring the gravel sometime soon,' he said.

She watched him crossing the highway. Then automatically she climbed out of the pit.

She was mounting the tedious stone steps behind him. Her jaw was clamped shut, and her face had gone white with anger. He had not turned around once to look at her. As they were nearing the top it occurred to her that he would rush into the house and slam the door in her face. Hurriedly she climbed three steps at once so as to be directly behind him. When he opened the door, she pushed across the threshold with him; he did not seem to notice her at all. Inside the dimly lit vestibule the smell of fresh paint was very strong. After a few seconds her eyes became more accustomed to the light, and she saw that the square room was packed solid with furniture. The boy was already pushing his way between two identical bureaux which stood back to back. The space between them was so narrow that she feared she would not be able to follow him. She looked around frantically for a wider artery, but seeing that there was none, she squeezed between the bureaux, pinching her flesh painfully, until she reached a free space at the other end. Here the furniture was less densely packed—in fact, three armchairs had been shoved together around an uncluttered area, wide enough to provide leg room for three people, providing they did not mind a tight squeeze. To her left a door opened on to total darkness. She expected him to rush headlong out of the room into the dark in a final attempt to escape her, but to her astonishment he threaded his way carefully in the opposite direction until he reached the circle of chairs. He entered it and sat down in one of them. After a second's hesitation, she followed his example.

The chair was deeper and softer than any she had ever sat in before. She tickled the thick velvet arms with her finger tips. Here and there, they grazed a stiff area where the nap had worn thin. The paint fumes were making her eyes smart, and she was beginning to feel apprehensive. She had forgotten to consider that grown people would probably be in the house, but now she gazed uneasily into the dark space through the open door opposite her. It was cold in the vestibule, and despite her woollen coat she began to shiver.

'If he would tell me now where he comes from,' she said to herself, 'then I could go away before anybody else came.' Her anger had vanished, but she could not bring herself to speak aloud, or even to turn around and look at him. He sat so still that it was hard for her to believe he was actually beside her in his chair.

Without warning, the dark space opposite her was lighted up. Her heart sank as she stared at a green wall, still shiny with wet paint. It hurt her eyes. A woman stepped into the visible area, her heels sounding on the floorboards. She was wearing a print dress and over it a long brown sweater which obviously belonged to a man.

'Are you there, Franklin?' she called out, and she walked into the vestibule and switched on a second light. She stood still and looked at him.

'I thought I heard you come in,' she said. Her voice was flat, and her posture at that moment did not inspire Mary with respect. 'Come to visit Franklin?' she asked, as if suddenly aware that her son was not alone. 'I think I'll visit too for a while.' She advanced toward them. When she reached the circle she squeezed in and sat opposite Mary.

'I hoped we'd get a visit or two while we were here,' she said to her. 'That's why I arranged this little sitting place. All the rest of the rooms are being painted, or else they're still too smelly for visiting. Last time we were here we didn't see anyone for the whole two weeks. But he was a baby then. I thought maybe this time he'd contact when he went out. He goes out a lot of the day.' She glanced at her son. 'You've got some dirt on that chair,' she remarked in a tone which did not express the slightest disapproval. She turned back to Mary. 'I'd rather have a girl than a boy,' she said. 'There's nothing much I can discuss with a boy. A grown woman isn't interested in the same things a boy is interested in.' She scratched a place below her shoulder blades. 'My preference is discussing furnishings. Always has been. I like that better than I like discussing styles. I'll discuss styles if the company wants to, but I don't enjoy it nearly so well. The only thing about furnishings that leaves me cold is curtains. I never was interested in curtains, even when I was young. I like lamps about the best. Do you?'

Mary was huddling as far back into her chair as

she could, but even so, without drawing her legs up and sitting on her feet, it was impossible to avoid physical contact with the woman, whose knees lightly touched hers every time she shifted a little in her chair. Inwardly, too, Mary shrank from her. She had never before been addressed so intimately by a grown person. She closed her eyes, seeking the dark gulf that always had separated her from the adult world. And she clutched the seat cushion hard, as if she were afraid of being wrenched from the chair.

'We came here six years ago,' the woman continued, 'when the Speeds had their house painted, and now they're having it painted again, so we're here again. They can't be in the house until it's good and dry because they've both got nose trouble—both the old man and the old lady—but we're not related. Only by marriage. I'm a kind of relative to them, but not enough to be really classed as a relative. Just enough so that they'd rather have me come and look after the house than a stranger. They gave me a present of money last time, but this time it'll be clothes for the boy. There's nothing to boys' clothes really. They don't mean anything.'

She sighed and looked around her.

'Well,' she said, 'we would like them to ask us over here more often than they do. Our town is way smaller than this, way smaller, but you can get all the same stuff there that you can here, if you've got the money to pay. I mean groceries and clothing and appliances.

We've got all that. As soon as the walls are dry we go back. Franklin doesn't want to. He don't like his home because he lives in an apartment; it's in the business section. He sits in a lot and don't go out and contact at all.'

The light shone through Mary's tightly closed lids. In the chair next to her there was no sound of a body stirring. She opened her eyes and looked down. His ankles were crossed and his feet were absolutely still.

'Franklin,' the woman said, 'get some candy for me and the girl.'

When he had gone she turned to Mary. 'He's not a rough boy like the others,' she said. 'I don't know what I'd do if he was one of the real ones with all the trimmings. He's got some girl in him, thank the Lord. I couldn't handle one of the real ones.'

He came out of the freshly painted room carrying a box.

'We keep our candy in tea boxes. We have for years, the woman said. 'They're good conservers.' She shrugged her shoulders. 'What more can you expect? Such is life.' She turned to her son. 'Open it and pass it to the girl first. Then me.'

The orange box was decorated with seated women and temples. Mary recognized it; her mother used the same tea at home. He slipped off the two rubber bands that held the cover on, and offered her the open box. With stiff fingers she took a stick of green candy from the top; she did not raise her eyes.

A few minutes later she was running alone down the stone steps. It was almost night, but the sky was faintly green near the horizon. She crossed the highway and stood on the hill only a few feet away from the pit. Far below her, lights were twinkling in the Polish section. Down there the shacks were stacked one against the other in a narrow strip of land between the lower road and the river.

After gazing down at the sparkling lights for a while, she began to breathe more easily. She had never experienced the need to look at things from a distance before, nor had she felt the relief that it can bring. All at once, the air stirring around her head seemed delightful; she drank in great draughts of it, her eyes fixed on the lights below.

'This isn't the regular air from up here that I'm breathing,' she said to herself. 'It's the air from down there. It's a trick I can do.'

She felt her blood tingle as it always did whenever she scored a victory, and she needed to score several of them in the course of each day. This time she was defeating the older woman.

The following afternoon, even though it was raining hard, her mother could not stop her from going out, but she had promised to keep her hood buttoned and not to sit on the ground.

The stone steps were running with water. She sat down and looked into the enveloping mist, a fierce light in her eyes. Her fingers twitched nervously, deep in the recesses of her rubber pockets. It was unbelievable that they should not at any moment encounter something wonderful and new, unbelievable, too, that he should be ignorant of her love for him. Surely he knew that all the while his mother was talking, she in secret had been claiming him for her own. He would come out soon to join her on the steps, and they would go away together.

Hours later, stiff with cold, she stood up. Even had he remained all day at the window he could never have sighted her through the heavy mist. She knew this, but she could never climb the steps to fetch him; that was impossible. She ran headlong down the stone steps and across the highway. When she reached the pit she stopped dead and stood with her feet in the soft clay mud, panting for breath.

'Men,' she said after a minute, 'men, I told you we were going to specialize.' She stopped abruptly, but it was too late. She had, for the first time in her life, spoken to her men before summoning them to order with a bugle call. She was shocked, and her heart beat hard against her ribs, but she went on. 'We're going to be the only outfit in the world that can do real mountain goat fighting.' She closed her eyes, seeking the dark gulf again; this time she needed to hear the men's hearts beating, more clearly than her own. A car was sounding its horn on the highway. She looked up.

'We can't climb those stone steps up there.' She was

shouting and pointing at the house. 'No outfit can, no outfit ever will. . . .' She was desperate. 'It's not for outfits. It's a flight of steps that's not for outfits . . . because it's . . . because. . . .' The reason was not going to come to her. She had begun to cheat now, and she knew it would never come.

She turned her cold face away from the pit, and without dismissing her men, crept down the hill.

ANDREW

Andrew's mother looked at her son's face. 'He wants to get away from us,' she thought, 'and he will.' She felt overcome by a mortal fatigue. 'He simply wants to spring out of his box into the world.' With a flippant and worldly gesture she described a flight through the air. Then abruptly she burst into tears and buried her face in her hands.

Andrew watched her thin shoulders shaking inside her woollen dress. When his mother cried he felt as though his face were made of marble. He could not accept the weeping as a part of her personality. It did not appear to be the natural climax of a mood. Instead it seemed to descend upon her from somewhere far away, as if she were giving voice to the crying of a child in some distant place. For it was the crying of a creature many years younger then she, a disgrace for which he felt responsible, since it was usually because of him that she cried.

There was nothing he could say to console her because she was right. He wanted to go away, and there was nothing else he wanted at all. 'It's natural when you're young to want to go away,' he would say to himself, but it did not help; he always felt that his own desire to escape was different from that of others. When he was in a good humor he would go about feeling that he and many others too were *all* going away. On such days his face was smooth and he enjoyed his life, although even then he was not communicative. More than anything he wanted all days to be like those rare free ones when he went about whistling and enjoying every simple thing he did. But he had to work hard to get such days, because of his inner conviction that his own going away was like no other going away in the world, a certainty he found it impossible to dislodge. He was right, of course, but from a very early age his life had been devoted to his struggle to rid himself of his feeling of uniqueness. With the years he was becoming more expert at travesty, so that now his mother's crying was more destructive. Watching her cry now, he was more convinced than ever that he was not like other boys who wanted to go away. The truth bit into him harder, for seeing her he could not believe even faintly that he shared his sin with other young men. He and his mother were isolated, sharing the same disgrace, and because of this sharing, separated from one another. His life was truly miserable compared to the lives of other boys, and he knew it.

When his mother's sobs had quieted down somewhat, his father called the waitress and asked for the check. 'That's good tomato soup,' he told her. 'And ham with Hawaiian pineapple is one of my favorites, as you know.' The waitress did not answer, and the engaging expression on his face slowly faded.

They pushed their chairs back and headed for the cloakroom. When they were outside Andrew's father suggested that they walk to the summit of the sloping lawn where some cannonballs were piled in the shape of a pyramid. 'We'll go over to the cannonballs,' he said. 'Then we'll come back.'

They struggled up the hill in the teeth of a bitterly cold wind, holding on to their hats. 'This is the north, folks!' his father shouted into the gale. 'It's hard going at times but in a hot climate no one develops.'

Andrew put his foot against one of the cannonballs. He could feel the cold iron through the sole of his shoe.

He had applied for a job in a garage, but he was inducted into the Army before he knew whether or not they had accepted his application. He loved being in the Army, and even took pleasure in the nickname which his hutmates had given him the second day after his arrival. He was called Buttonlip; because of this name he talked even less than usual. In general he hated to talk and could not imagine talking as being a natural expression of a man's thoughts. This was not shyness, but secretiveness.

One day in the Fall he set out on a walk through the pine grove surrounding the camp. Soon he sniffed smoke and stopped walking. 'Someone's making a fire,' he said to himself. Then he continued on his way. It was dusk in the grove, but beyond, outside, the daylight was still bright. Very shortly he reached a clearing. A young soldier sat there, crouched over a fire which he was feeding with long twigs. Andrew thought he recognized him – he too was undoubtedly a recent arrival – and so his face was not altogether unfamiliar.

The boy greeted Andrew with a smile and pointed to a tree trunk that lay on the ground nearby. 'Sit down,' he said. 'I'm going to cook dinner. The mess sergeant gives me my stuff uncooked when I want it that way so I can come out here and make a campfire.'

Andrew had an urge to bolt from the clearing, but he seated himself stiffly on the end of the tree trunk. The boy was beautiful, with an Irish-American face and thick curly brown hair. His cheeks were blood red from the heat of the flames. Andrew looked at his face and fell in love with him. Then he could not look away.

A mess kit and a brown paper package lay on the ground. 'My food is there in that brown bag,' the boy said. 'I'll give you a little piece of meat so you can see how good it tastes when it's cooked here, out in the air. Did you go in for bonfires when you were a kid?'

'No,' said Andrew. 'Too much wind,' he added, some vague memory stirring in his mind.

'There's lots of wind,' he agreed, and Andrew was unreasonably delighted that the boy considered his remark a sensible one. 'Lots of wind, but that never need stop you.' He looked up at Andrew with a bright smile. 'Not if you like a fire and the outdoors. Where I worked they used to call me Outdoor Tommy. Nobody got sore.'

Andrew was so disarmed by his charm that he did not find the boy's last statement odd until he had heard the sentence repeated several times inside his head.

'Sore?'

'Yes, sore.' He untied the string that bound his food package and set the meat on a little wire grate. 'They never got sore at me,' he repeated, measuring his words. 'They were a right nice bunch. Sometimes guys don't take to it if you like something real well. They get sore. These guys didn't get sore. Never. They saw me going off to the woods with my supper every evening, and sometimes even, one or two of them would come along. And sometimes twenty-five of us would go out with steaks. But mostly I just went by myself and they stayed back playing games in the cottages or going into town. If it had been winter I'd have stayed in the cottages more. I was never there in winter. If I had been, I might have gone out anyway. I like to make a fire in the snow.'

'Where were you?' asked Andrew.

'In a factory by a stream.' The meat was cooked, and he cut off a tiny piece for Andrew. 'This is all you're going to get. Otherwise I won't have enough in me.'

'I've eaten. With the others,' said Andrew shortly.

'You've got to try this,' the boy insisted. 'And see if you like eating it this way, cooked on the coals outdoors. Then maybe you can get on the good side of the mess sergeant and bring your food out here, too. They're all right here. I could stay in this outfit. Just as good as I could stay back home in the hotel.'

'You live in a hotel?'

'I lived in a hotel except the summer I was in the factory.'

'Well, I'll see you,' Andrew mumbled, walking away.

One night after he had eaten his supper he found himself wandering among the huts on the other side of the mess hall. It was Saturday night and most of the huts were dark. He was dejected, and thought of going into town and drinking beer by himself. Andrew drank only beer because he considered other forms of alcohol too expensive, although most of the other soldiers, who had less money than he, drank whiskey. As he walked along thinking of the beer he heard a voice calling to him. He looked up and saw Tommy standing in the doorway of a hut only a few feet away. They greeted each other, and Tommy motioned to him to wait. Then he went inside to get something.

Andrew leaned against a tree with his hands in

his pockets. When Tommy came out he held a flat box in his hand. 'Sparklers,' he said. 'I bought them after the Fourth, cut-rate. It's the best time to buy them.'

'That's good to know,' said Andrew. He had never touched fireworks except on the day of the Fourth. He had a brief memory of alleys on summer nights, where boys were grinding red devils under their heels in the dark. Compared to him they were poor, and he was therefore, like all well-off children, both revolted by them and envious of them. The fact that they played with fireworks after the Fourth of July was disgusting in a way. It had a foreign flavor, and made him feel a little sick, just as the Irish did, and the Jews, and circus people. But he was also excited by them. The sick feeling was part of the excitement.

Andrew had never dressed as a ragamuffin on Thanksgiving, and he had once almost fainted when two boys disguised as hags had come begging at the door. His father's rage had contributed greatly to the nightmarish quality of the memory. It was usually his mother, and not his father, who was angry. But he remembered that his father had seemed to attach great importance to the custom of masquerading on Thanksgiving. 'He should be dressed up himself and out there with the others!' he had cried. 'He has no right to be lying there, white as a sheet. There's no earthly reason for it. This is a holiday. It's time for *fun*. My God, doesn't anyone in the house ever have any fun? I was a ragamuffin every year until I was grown. Why doesn't he tear up an old pair of pants and go out? I'll take the crown out of my straw hat if he wants to wear it. But he should go out!'

Quite naturally Andrew had thought of running away. This was one of his worst memories. He hated to hear his father speak about the poor. His own romantic conception of them made his father's democratic viewpoint unacceptable. It was as incongruous as if he had come into the parlor and found his father offering one of his cigarettes to a pirate or a gypsy. He preferred his mother's disdain for the poor. In fact, she liked nothing but the smell of her intimates. Of course, she made him feel sick, too, but sick in a different way.

'Come on. Take one,' Tommy was saying, and he lighted a sparkler. Andrew stared at the needle-like sparks. The hissing sound of the sparkler awakened old sick feelings, and he longed to pull the little stick from between Tommy's fingers and bury the bright sparks in the earth. Instead, he looked gloomy and said nothing. He liked the fact that Tommy was poor, but he did not want him to be so poor that he seemed foreign. Then he realized that others might not see a connection between being a foreigner and playing with sparklers after the Fourth of July, and he was aware that there was really no logical connection. Yet he himself felt that there was one. Sometimes he wondered whether or not other people went about pretending to be logical while actually they felt as he did inside, but this was not very often, since he usually took it for granted that everyone was more honest than he. The fact that it was impossible to say anything of all this to Tommy both depressed and irritated him.

'I saved a whole box of sparklers for you,' Tommy said. 'I thought you'd be coming to the clearing.'

Andrew could not believe he was hearing the words. At the same time his heart had begun to beat faster. He told himself that he must retain a natural expression.

'I don't know if you like to fool around with stuff they make for kids,' Tommy went on. 'Maybe you think it's not worth your while. But you don't have to pay much attention to these. You light 'em and they burn themselves out. You can swing 'em around and talk at the same time. Or you don't even have to swing 'em. You can stick 'em in the ground and they go on all by themselves, like little pinwheels. There's not much point to 'em, but I get 'em anyway, every summer after the Fourth of July is over with. This isn't the box I saved for you. That one I gave to someone else who had a nephew.' He handed the box to Andrew.

Andrew's face was like stone and his mouth was drawn.

'Here.' Tommy tapped the back of Andrew's hand with the flat box. 'Here are your sparklers.'

'No,' said Andrew. 'I don't want any sparklers.' He was not going to offer any explanation for refusing them. Tommy did not seem to want one in any case. He went on tracing designs in the night with his sparkler. 'I'll just stash this box away if you don't want 'em. I can use 'em up. It's better to have one of these going than nothing, and sometimes there's no time for me to build a bonfire.'

'You take things easy, don't you?' Andrew said.

EMMY MOORE'S JOURNAL

On certain days I forget why I'm here. Today once again I wrote my husband all my reasons for coming. He encouraged me to come each time I was in doubt. He said that the worst danger for me was a state of vagueness, so I wrote telling him why I had come to the Hotel Henry – my eighth letter on this subject – but with each new letter I strengthen my position. I am reproducing the letter here. Let there be no mistake. My journal is intended for publication. I want to publish for glory, but also in order to aid other women. This is the letter to my husband, Paul Moore, to whom I have been married sixteen years. (I am childless.) He is of North Irish descent, and a very serious lawyer. Also a solitary and lover of the country. He knows all mushrooms, bushes and trees, and he is interested in geology. But these interests do not exclude me. He is sympathetic towards me, and kindly. He wants very much for me to be happy, and worries because I am not. He knows everything about me, including how much I deplore being the feminine kind of woman that I am. In fact, I am unusually feminine for an American of Anglo stock. (Born in Boston.) I am almost a 'Turkish' type. Not physically, at least not entirely, because though fat I have ruddy Scotch cheeks and my eyes are round and not slanted or almond-shaped. But sometimes I feel certain that I exude an atmosphere very similar to theirs (the Turkish women's) and then I despise myself. I find the women in my country so extraordinarily manly and independent, capable of leading regiments, or of fending for themselves on desert islands if necessary. (These are poor examples, but I am getting my point across.) For me it is an experience simply to have come here alone to the Hotel Henry and to eat my dinner and lunch by myself. If possible before I die, I should like to become a little more independent, and a little less Turkish than I am now. Before I go any further, I had better say immediately that I mean no offense to Turkish women. They are probably busy combating the very same Turkish quality in themselves that I am controlling in me. I understand, too (though this is irrelevant), that many Turkish women are beautiful, and I think that they have discarded their veils. Any other American woman would be sure of this. She would know one way or the other whether the veils had been discarded, whereas I am afraid to come out with a definite statement. I have a feeling that they really have got rid of their veils, but I won't swear to it. Also, if they have done so, I have no idea when they did. Was it many years ago or recently?

Here is my letter to Paul Moore, my husband, in which there is more about Turkish women. Since I am writing this journal with a view to publication, I do not want to ramble on as though I had all the space in the world. No publisher will attempt printing an *enormous* journal written by an unknown woman. It would be too much of a financial risk. Even I, with my ignorance of all matters pertaining to business, know this much. But they may print a small one.

My letter (written yesterday, the morrow of my drunken evening in the Blue Bonnet Room when I accosted the society salesman):

Dearest Paul:

I cannot simply live out my experiment here at the Hotel Henry without trying to justify or at least explain in letters my reasons for being here, and with fair regularity. You encouraged me to write whenever I felt I needed to clarify my thoughts. But you did tell me that I must not feel the need to *justify* my actions. However, I *do* feel the need to justify my actions, and I am certain that until the prayed-for metamorphosis has occurred I shall go on feeling just this need. Oh, how well I know that you would interrupt me at this point and warn me against expecting too much. So I shall say in lieu of metamorphosis, the prayed-for *improvement*. But until then I must justify myself every day. Perhaps you will get a letter every day. On some days the need to write lodges itself in my throat like a cry that must be uttered.

As for the Turkish problem, I am coming to it. You must understand that I am an admirer of Western civilization; that is, of the women who are members of this group. I feel myself that I fall short of being a member, that by some curious accident I was not born in Turkey but should have been. Because of my usual imprecision I cannot even tell how many countries belong to what we call Western Civilization, but I believe Turkey is the place where East meets

West, isn't it? I can just about imagine the women there, from what I have heard about the country and the pictures I have seen of it. As for being troubled or obsessed by real Oriental women, I am not. (I refer to the Chinese, Japanese, Hindus, and so on.) Naturally I am less concerned with the Far Eastern women because there is no danger of my being like them. (The Turkish women are just near enough.) The Far Eastern ones are so very far away, at the opposite end of the earth, that they could easily be just as independent and masculine as the women of the Western world. The ones living in-between the two masculine areas would be soft and feminine. Naturally I don't believe this for a minute, but still, the real Orientals are so far away and such a mystery to me that it might as well be true. Whatever they are, it couldn't affect me. They look too different from the way I look. Whereas Turkish women don't. (Their figures are exactly like mine, alas!)

Now I shall come to the point. I know full well that you will consider the above discourse a kind of joke. Or if you don't, you will be irritated with me for making statements of such a sweeping and inaccurate nature. For surely you will consider the picture of the world that I present as inaccurate. I myself know that this concept of the women (all three sets – Western, Middle and Eastern) is a puerile one. It could even be called downright idiotic. Yet I assure you that I see things this way, if I relax even a little and look through my own eyes into what is really inside my head. (Though because of my talent for mimicry I am able to simulate looking through the eyes of an educated person when I wish to.) Since I am giving you such a frank picture of myself, I may as well go the whole hog and admit to you that my secret picture of the world is grossly inaccurate. I have completely forgotten to include in it any of the Latin countries. (France, Italy, Spain.) For instance, I have jumped from the Anglo world to the semi-Oriental as if there were no countries in between at all. I know that these exist. (I have even lived in two of them.) But they do not fit into my scheme. I just don't think about the Latins very much, and this is less understandable than my not thinking about the Chinese or Javanese or Japanese women. You can see why without my having to explain it to you. I do know that the French women are more interested in sports than they used to be, and for all I know they may be indistinguishable from Anglo women by now. I haven't been to France recently so I can't be sure. But in any case the women of those countries don't enter into my picture of the world. Or shall I say that the fact of having forgotten utterly to consider them has not altered the way I visualize the division of the world's women? Incredible though it may seem to you, it hasn't altered anything. (My having forgotten all Latin countries, South America included.) I want you to know the whole truth about me. But don't imagine that I wouldn't be capable of concealing my ignorance from you if I wanted to. I am so wily and feminine that I could live by your side for a lifetime and deceive you afresh each day. But I will have no truck with feminine wiles. I know how they can absorb the hours of the day. Many women are delighted to sit around spinning their webs. It is an absorbing occupation, and the women feel they are getting somewhere. And so they are, but only for as long as the man is there to be deceived. And a wily woman alone is a pitiful sight to behold. Naturally.

I shall try to be honest with you so that I can live with you and yet won't be pitiful. Even if tossing my feminine tricks out the window means being left no better than an illiterate backwoodsman, or the bottom fish scraping along the ocean bed, I prefer to have it this way. Now I am too tired to write more. Though I don't feel that I have clarified enough or justified enough.

I shall write you soon about the effect the war has had upon me. I have spoken to you about it, but you have never seemed to take it very seriously. Perhaps seeing in black and white what I feel will affect your opinion of me. Perhaps you will leave me. I accept the challenge. My Hotel Henry experience includes this risk. I got drunk two nights ago. It's hard to believe that I am forty-seven, isn't it?

My love,
Emmy

Now that I have copied this letter into my journal (I had forgotten to make a carbon), I shall take my walk. My scheme included a few weeks of solitude at the Hotel Henry before attempting anything. I did not even intend to write in my journal as soon as I started to, but simply to sit about collecting my thoughts, waiting for the knots of habit to undo themselves. But after only week here – two nights ago – I felt amazingly alone and disconnected from my past life, so I began my journal.

My first interesting contact was the salesman in the Blue Bonnet Room. I had heard about this eccentric through my in-laws, the Moores, before I ever came up here. My husband's cousin Laurence Moore told me about him when he heard I was coming. He said: 'Take a walk through Grey and Bottle's Department Store, and you'll see a man with a lean red face and reddish hair selling materials by the bolt. That man has an income and is related to Hewitt Molain. He doesn't need to work. He was in my fraternity. Then he disappeared. The next I heard of him he was working there at Grey and Bottle's. I stopped by and said hello to him. For a nut he seemed like a very decent chap. You might even have a drink with him. I think he's quite up to general conversation.'

I did not mention Laurence Moore to the society salesman because I thought it might irritate him. I lied and pretended to have been here for months, when actually this is still only my second week at the Hotel Henry. I want everyone to think I have been here a long time. Surely it is not to impress them. Is there anything impressive about a lengthy stay at the Hotel Henry? Any sane person would be alarmed that I should even ask such a question. I ask it because deep in my heart I *do* think a lengthy stay at the Hotel Henry is impressive. Very easy to see that I would, and even sane of me to think it impressive, but not sane of me to expect anyone else to think so, particularly a stranger. Perhaps I simply like to hear myself telling it. I hope so. I shall write some more tomorrow, but now I must go out. I am going to buy a supply of cocoa. When I'm not drunk I like to have a cup of cocoa before going to sleep. My husband likes it too.

She could not stand the overheated room a second longer. With some difficulty she raised the window, and the cold wind blew in. Some loose sheets of paper went skimming off the top of the desk and flattened themselves against the bookcase. She shut the window and they fell to the floor. The cold air had changed her mood. She looked down at the sheets of paper. They were part of the letter she had just copied. She picked them up: '*I don't feel that I have clarified enough or justified enough*,' she read. She closed her eyes and shook her head. She had been so happy copying this letter into her journal, but now her heart was faint as she scanned its scattered pages. 'I have said nothing,' she muttered to herself in alarm. 'I have said nothing at all. I have not clarified my reasons for being at the Hotel Henry. I have not justified myself.'

Automatically she looked around the room. A bottle of whiskey stood on the floor beside one of the legs of the bureau. She stepped forward, picked it up by the neck, and settled with it into her favorite wicker chair.

GOING TO MASSACHUSETTS

Bozoe rubbed away some tears with a closed fist.

'Come on, Bozoe,' said Janet. 'You're not going to the North Pole.'

Bozoe tugged at the woolly fur, and pulled a little of it out.

'Leave your coat alone,' said Janet.

'I don't remember why I'm going to Massachusetts,' Bozoe moaned. 'I knew it would be like this, once I got to the station.'

'If you don't want to go to Massachusetts,' said Janet, 'then come on back to the apartment. We'll stop at Fanny's on the way. I want to buy those tumblers made out of knobby glass. I want brown ones.'

Bozoe started to cry in earnest. This caused Janet considerable embarrassment. She was conscious of herself as a public figure because the fact that she owned and ran a garage had given her a good deal of publicity not only in East Clinton but in the neighboring counties. This scene, she said to herself, makes us look like two Italians saying goodbye. Everybody'll think we're Italians. She did not feel true sympathy for Bozoe. Her sense of responsibility was overdeveloped, but she was totally lacking in real tenderness.

'There's no reason for you to cry over a set of whiskey tumblers,' said Janet. 'I told you ten days ago that I was going to buy them.'

'Passengers boarding Bus Number Twenty-seven, north-bound. . . .'

'I'm not crying about whiskey tumblers.' Bozoe managed with difficulty to get the words out. 'I'm crying about Massachusetts. I can't remember my reasons.'

'Rockport, Rayville, Muriel. . . .'

'Why don't you listen to the loudspeaker, Bozoe? It's giving you information. If you paid attention to what's going on around you you'd be a lot better off. You concentrate too much on your own private affairs. Try more to be a part of the world.'

'. . . *The truth is that I am only twenty-five miles away from the apartment, as you have probably guessed. In fact, you could not help but guess it, since you are perfectly familiar with Larry's Bar and Grill. I could not go to Massachusetts. I cried the whole way up to Muriel and it was as if someone else were getting off the bus, not myself. But someone who was in a desperate hurry to reach the next stop. I was in mortal terror that the bus would not stop at Muriel but continue on to some further destination where I would not know any familiar face. My terror was so great that I actually stopped crying. I kept from crying all the way. That is a lie. Not an actual lie because I never lie as you know. Small solace to either one of us, isn't it? I am sure that you would prefer me to lie, rather than be so intent on explaining my dilemma to you night and day. I am convinced that you would prefer me to lie. It would give you more time for the garage.*'

'So?' queried Sis McEvoy, an unkind note in her voice. To Janet she did not sound noticeably unkind, since Sis McEvoy was habitually sharp-sounding, and like her had very little sympathy for other human beings. She was sure that Sis McEvoy was bad, and she was determined to save her. She was going to save her quietly without letting Sis suspect her determination. Janet did everything secretly; in fact, secrecy was the essence of her nature, and from it she derived her pleasure and her sense of being an important member of society.

'What's it all about?' Sis asked irritably. 'Why doesn't she raise kids or else go to a psychologist or a psychoanalyst or whatever? My ovaries are crooked or I'd raise kids myself. That's what God's after, isn't it? Space ships or no space ships. What's the problem, anyway? How are her ovaries and the rest of the mess?'

Janet smiled mysteriously. Bozoe has never wanted a child,' she said. 'She told me she was too scared.'

'Don't you despise cowards?' said Sis. 'Jesus Christ, they turn my stomach.'

Janet frowned. 'Bozoe says she despises cowards, too. She worries herself sick about it. She's got it all linked up together with Heaven and Hell. She thinks so much about Heaven and Hell that she's useless. I've told her for years to occupy herself. I've told her that God would like her better if she was occupied. But she says God isn't interested. That's a kind of slam at me, I suppose. At me and the garage. She's got it in for the garage. It doesn't bother me, but it makes me a little sore when she tries to convince me that I wouldn't be interested in the garage unless she talked to me day and night about her troubles. As if I was interested in the garage just out of spite. I'm a normal woman and I'm interested in my work, like all women are in modern times. I'm a little stockier than most, I guess, and not fussy or feminine. That's because my father was my ideal and my mother was an alcoholic. I'm stocky and I don't like pretty dresses and I'm interested in my work. My work is like God to me. I don't mean I put it above Him, but the next thing to Him. I have a feeling that he approves of my working. That he approves of my working in a garage. Maybe that's cheeky of me, but I can't help it. I've made a name for myself in the garage and I'm decent. I'm normal.' She paused for a moment to fill the two whiskey tumblers.

'Do you like my whiskey tumblers?' She was being unusually spry and talkative. 'I don't usually have much time to buy stuff. But I had to, of course. Bozoe never bought anything in her life. She's what you'd call a dead weight. She's getting fatter, too, all the time.'

'They're good tumblers,' said Sis McEvoy. 'They hold a lot of whiskey.'

Janet flushed slightly at the compliment. She atttributed the unaccustomed excitement she felt to her freedom from the presence of Bozoe Flanner.

'Bozoe was very thin when I first knew her,' she told Sis. 'And she didn't show any signs that she was going to sit night and day making up problems and worrying about God and asking me questions. There wasn't any of that in the beginning. Mainly she was meek, I guess, and she had soft-looking eyes, like a doe or a calf. Maybe she had the problems the whole time and was just planning to spring them on me later. I don't know. I never thought she was going to get so tied up in knots, or so fat either. Naturally if she were heavy and happy too it would be better.'

'I have no flesh on my bones at all,' said Sis McEvoy, as if she had not even heard the rest of the conversation. 'The whole family's thin, and every last one of us has a rotten lousy temper inherited from both sides. My father and my mother had rotten tempers.'

'I don't mind if you have a temper display in my apartment,' said Janet. 'Go to it. I believe in people expressing themselves. If you've inherited a temper there isn't much you can do about it except express it. I think it's much better for you to break this crockery pumpkin, for instance, than to hold your temper in and become unnatural. For instance, I could buy another pumpkin and you'd feel relieved. I'd gather that, at any rate. I don't know much about people, really. I never dabbled in people. They were never my specialty. But surely if you've inherited a temper from both sides it would seem to me that you would have to express it. It isn't your fault, is it, after all?' Janet seemed determined to show admiration for Sis McEvoy.

'I'm having fun,' she continued unexpectedly. 'It's a long time since I've had any fun. I've been too busy getting the garage into shape. Then there's Bozoe trouble. I've kept to the routine. Late Sunday breakfast with popovers and home-made jam. She eats maybe six of them, but with the same solemn expression on her face. I'm husky but a small eater. We have record players and television. But nothing takes her mind off herself. There's no point in my getting any more machines. I've got the cash and the good will, but there's absolutely no point.'

'You seem to be very well set up,' said Sis McEvoy, narrowing her eyes. 'Here's to you.' She tipped her glass and drained it.

Janet filled Sister's glass at once. 'I'm having a whale of a good time,' she said. 'I hope you are. Of course I don't want to butt into your business. Bozoe always thought I pored over my account books for such a long time on purpose. She thought I was purposely trying to get away from her. What do you think, Sis McEvoy?' She asked this almost in a playful tone that bordered on a yet unexpressed flirtatiousness.

'I'm not interested in women's arguments with

each other,' said Sis at once. 'I'm interested in women's arguments with men. What else is there? The rest doesn't amount to a row of monkeys.'

'Oh, I agree,' Janet said, as if she were delighted by this statement which might supply her with the stimulus she was after. 'I agree one thousand percent. Remember I spend more time in the garage with the men than I do with Bozoe Flanner.'

'I'm not actually living with my husband because of my temper,' said Sis. 'I don't like long-standing relationships. They disagree with me. I get the blues. I don't want anyone staying in my life for a long time. It gives me the creeps. Men are crazy about me. I like the cocktails and the compliments. Then after a while they turn my stomach.'

'You're a very interesting woman,' Janet Murphy announced, throwing caution to the winds and finding it pleasant.

'I know I'm interesting,' said Sis. 'But I'm not so sure life is interesting.'

'Are you interested in money?' Janet asked her. 'I don't mean money for the sake of money, but for buying things.'

Sis did not answer, and Janet feared that she had been rude. 'I didn't mean to hurt your feelings,' she said. 'After all, money comes up in everybody's life. Even duchesses have to talk about money. But I won't, any more. Come on. Let's shake.' She held out her hand to Sis McEvoy, but Sis allowed it to stay there foolishly, without accepting the warm grip Janet had intended for her.

'I'm really sorry,' she went on, 'if you think I was trying to be insulting and personal. I honestly was not. The fact is that I have been so busy building up a reputation for the garage that I behave like a savage. I'll never mention money again.' In her heart she felt that Sis was somehow pleased that the subject had been brought up, but was not yet ready to admit it. Sis's tedious work at the combination tearoom and soda fountain where they had met could scarcely make her feel secure.

Bozoe doesn't play one single feminine trick, she told herself, and after all, after struggling nearly ten years to build up a successful and unusual business I'm entitled to some returns. I'm in a rut with Bozoe and this Sis is going to get me out of it. (By now she was actually furious with Bozoe.) I'm entitled to some fun. The men working for me have more fun than I have.

'I feel grateful to you, Sis,' she said without explaining her remark. 'You've done me a service. May I tell you that I admire your frankness, without offending you?'

Sis McEvoy was beginning to wonder if Janet were another nut like Bozoe Flanner. This worried her a little, but she was too drunk by now for clear thinking. She was enjoying the compliments, although it was disturbing that they should be coming from a woman. She was very proud of never having been depraved or abnormal, and pleased to be merely mean and discontented to the extent of not having been able to stay with any man for longer than the three months she had spent with her husband.

'I'll read you more of Bozoe's letter,' Janet suggested.

'I can't wait,' said Sis. 'I can't wait to hear a lunatic's mind at work first-hand. Her letter's so cheerful and elevating. And so constructive. Go to it. But fill my glass first so I can concentrate. I'd hate to miss a word. It would kill me.'

Janet realized that it was unkind of her to be reading her friend's letter to someone who so obviously had only contempt for it. But she felt no loyalty – only eagerness to make Sis see how hard her life had been. She felt that in this way the bond between them might be strengthened.

'Well, here it comes,' she said. 'Stop me when you can't stand it any more. *I know that you expected me to come back. You did not feel I had the courage to carry out my scheme. I still expect to work it out. But not yet. I am more than ever convinced that my salvation lies in solitude, and coming back to the garage before I have even reached Massachusetts would be a major defeat for me, as I'm sure you must realize, even though you pretend not to know what I'm talking about most of the time. I am convinced that you do know what I'm talking about and if you pretend ignorance of my dilemma so you can increase efficiency at the garage you are going to defeat yourself. I can't actually save you, but I can point little things out to you constantly. I refer to your soul, naturally, and not to any success you've had or to your determination. In any case it came to me on the bus that it was not time for me to leave you, and that although going to Massachusetts required more courage and strength than I seemed able to muster, I was at the same time being very selfish in going. Selfish because I was thinking in terms of my salvation and not yours. I'm glad I thought of this. It is why I stopped crying and got off the bus. Naturally you would disapprove, because I had paid for my ticket which is now wasted, if for no other reason. That's the kind of thing you like me to think about, isn't it? It makes you feel that I'm more human. I have never admired being human, I must say. I want to be like God. But I haven't begun yet. First I have to go to Massachusetts and be alone. But I got off the bus. And I've wasted the fare. I can hear you stressing that above all else, as I say. But I want you to understand that it was not cowardice alone that stopped me from going to Massachusetts. I don't feel that I can allow you to sink into the mire of contentment and happy ambitious enterprise. It is my duty to prevent you from it as much as I do for myself. It is not fair of me to go away until you completely understand how I feel about God and my destiny. Surely we have been brought together for some purpose, even if that purpose ends by our being separate again. But not until the time is ripe. Naturally, the psychiatrists would at once declare that I was laboring under a compulsion. I am violently against psychiatry, and, in fact, against happiness. Though of course I love it. I love happiness, I mean. Of course you would not believe this. Naturally darling I love you, and I'm afraid that if you don't start suffering soon God will take some terrible vengeance. It is better for you to offer yourself. Don't accept social or financial security as your final aim. Or fame in the garage. Fame is unworthy of you; that is, the desire for it. Janet, my beloved, I do not expect you to be gloomy or fanatical as I am. I do not believe that God intended you for quite as harrowing a destiny as He did for me. I don't mean this as an insult. I believe you should actually thank your stars. I would really like to be fulfilling humble daily chores myself and listening to a concert at night or television or playing a card game. But I can find no rest, and I don't think you should either. At least not until you have fully understood my dilemma on earth. That means that you must no longer turn a deaf ear to me and pretend that your preoccupation with the garage is in a sense a holier absorption than trying to understand and fully realize the importance and meaning of my dilemma. I think that you hear more than you admit, too. There is a stubborn streak in your nature working against you, most likely unknown to yourself. An insistence on being shallow rather than profound. I repeat: I do not expect you to be as profound as I am. But to insist on exploiting the most shallow side of one's nature, out of stubbornness and merely because it is more pleasant to be shallow, is certainly a sin. Sis McEvoy will help you to express the shallow side of your nature, by the way. Like a toboggan slide.'*

Janet stopped abruptly, appalled at having read this last part aloud. She had not expected Bozoe to mention Sis at all. 'Gee,' she said. 'Gosh! She's messing everything up together. I'm awfully sorry.'

Sis McEvoy stood up and walked unsteadily to the television set. Some of her drink slopped onto the rug as she went. She faced Janet with fierce eyes. 'There's nobody in the world who can talk to me like that, and there's not going to be. Never!' She was leaning on the set and steadying herself against it with both hands. 'I'll keep on building double-decker sandwiches all my life first. It's five flights to the top of the building where I live. It's an insurance building, life insurance, and I'm the only woman who lives there. I have boy friends come when they want to. I don't have to worry, either. I'm crooked so I don't have to bother with abortions or any other kind of mess. The hell with television anyway.'

She likes the set, Janet said to herself. She felt more secure. 'Bozoe and I don't have the same opinions at all,' she said. 'We don't agree on anything.'

'Who cares? You live in the same apartment, don't you? You've lived in the same apartment for ten years. Isn't that all anybody's got to know?' She rapped with her fist on the wood panelling of the television set. 'Whose is it, anyhow?' She was growing increasingly aggressive.

'It's mine,' Janet said. 'It's my television set.' She spoke loud so that Sis would be sure to catch her words.

'What the hell do I care?' cried Sis. 'I live on top of a life-insurance building and I work in a combination soda-fountain lunch-room. Now read me the rest of the letter.'

'I don't think you really want to hear any more of Bozoe's nonsense,' Janet said smoothly. 'She's spoiling our evening together. There's no reason for us to put up with it all. Why should we? Why don't I make something to eat? Not a sandwich. You must be sick of sandwiches.'

'What I eat is my own business,' Sis snapped.

'Naturally,' said Janet. 'I thought you might like something hot like bacon and eggs. Nice crisp bacon and eggs.' She hoped to persuade her so that she might forget about the letter.

'I don't like food,' said Sis. 'I don't even like millionaires' food, so don't waste your time.'

'I'm a small eater myself.' She had to put off reading Bozoe's letter until Sis had forgotten about it. 'My work at the garage requires some sustenance, of course. But it's brainwork now more than manual labor. Being a manager's hard on the brain.'

Sis looked at Janet and said: 'Your brain doesn't impress me. Or that garage. I like newspaper men. Men who are champions. Like champion boxers. I've known lots of champions. They take to me. Champions all fall for me, but I'd never want any of them to find out that I knew someone like your Bozoe. They'd lose their respect.'

'I wouldn't introduce Bozoe to a boxer either, or anybody else who was interested in sports. I know they'd be bored. I know.' She waited. 'You're very nice. Very intelligent. You *know* people. That's an asset.'

'Stay with Bozoe and her television set,' Sis growled.

'It's not her television set. It's mine, Sis. Why don't you sit down? Sit on the couch over there.'

'The apartment belongs to both of you, and so does the set. I know what kind of a couple you are. The whole world knows it. I could put you in jail if I wanted to. I could put you and Bozoe both in jail.'

In spite of these words she stumbled over to

the couch and sat down. 'Whiskey,' she demanded. 'The world loves drunks but it despises perverts. Athletes and boxers drink when they're not in training. All thc time.'

Janet went over to her and served her a glass of whiskey with very little ice. Let's hope she'll pass out, she said to herself. She couldn't see Sis managing the steps up to her room in the insurance building, and in any case she didn't want her to leave. She's such a relief after Bozoe, she thought. Alive and full of fighting spirit. She's much more my type, coming down to facts. She thought it unwise to go near Sis, and was careful to pour the fresh drink quickly and return to her own seat. She would have preferred to sit next to Sis, in spite of her mention of jail, but she did not relish being punched or smacked in the face. It's all Bozoe's fault, she said to herself. That's what she gets for thinking she's God. Her holy words can fill a happy peaceful room with poison from twenty-five miles away.

'I love my country,' said Sis, for no apparent reason. 'I love it to death!'

'Sure you do, Hon,' said Janet. 'I could murder Bozoe for upsetting you with her loony talk. You were so peaceful until she came in.'

'Read that letter,' said Sister. After a moment she repeated, as if from a distance: 'Read the letter.'

Janet was perplexed. Obviously food was not going to distract Sis, and she had nothing left to suggest, in any case, but some Gorton's Codfish made into cakes, and she did not dare to offer her these.

What a rumpus that would raise, she said to herself. And if I suggest turning on the television she'll raise the roof. Stay off television and codfish cakes until she's normal again. Working at a lunch counter is no joke.

There was nothing she could do but do as Sis told her and hope that she might fall asleep while she was reading her the letter. 'Damn Bozoe anyway,' she muttered audibly.

'Don't put on any acts,' said Sis, clearly awake. 'I hate liars and I always smell an act. Even though I didn't go to college. I have no respect for college.'

'I didn't go to college,' Janet began, hoping Sis might be led on to a new discussion. 'I went to commercial school.'

'Shut up, God damn you! Nobody ever tried to make a commercial school sound like an interesting topic except you. Nobody! You're out of your mind. Read the letter.'

'Just a second,' said Janet, knowing there was no hope for her. 'Let me put my glasses on and find my place. Doing accounts at the garage year in and year out has ruined my eyes. My eyes used to be perfect.' She added this last weakly, without hope of arousing either sympathy or interest.

Sis did not deign to answer.

'Well, here it is again,' she began apologetically. 'Here it is in all its glory.' She poured a neat drink to give herself courage. *'As I believe I just wrote you, I have been down to the bar and brought a drink back with me. (One more defeat for me, a defeat which is of course a daily occurrence, and I daresay I should not bother to mention it in this letter.) In any case I could certainly not face being without one after the strain of actually boarding the bus, even if I did get off without having the courage to stick on it until I got where I was going. However, please keep in mind the second reason I had for stopping short of my destination. Please read it over carefully so that you will not have only contempt for me. The part about the responsibility I feel toward you. The room here over Larry's Bar and Grill is dismal. It is one of several rented out by Larry's sister whom we met a year ago when we stopped here for a meal. You remember. It was the day we took Stretch for a ride and let him out of the car to run in the woods, that scanty patch of woods you found just as the sun was setting, and you kept picking up branches that were stuck together with wet leaves and dirt. . . .'*

THE IRON TABLE

They sat in the sun, looking out over a big new boulevard. The waiter had dragged an old iron table around from the other side of the hotel and set it down on the cement near a half-empty flower bed. A string stretched between stakes separated the hotel grounds from the sidewalk. Few of the guests staying at the hotel sat in the sun. The town was not a tourist center, and not many Anglo-Saxons came. Most of the guests were Spanish.

'The whole civilization is going to pieces,' he said.

Her voice was sorrowful. 'I know it.' Her

answers to his ceaseless complaining about the West's contamination of Moslem culture had become increasingly unpredictable. Today, because she felt that he was in a very irritable mood and in need of an argument, she automatically agreed with him. 'It's going to pieces so quickly, too,' she said, and her tone was sepulchral.

He looked at her without any light in his blue eyes. 'There are places where the culture has remained untouched,' he announced as if for the first time. 'If we went into the desert you wouldn't have to face all this. Wouldn't you love that?' He was punishing her for her swift agreement with him a moment earlier. He knew she had no desire to go to the desert, and that she believed it was not possible to continue trying to escape from the Industrial Revolution. Without realizing he was doing it he had provoked the argument he wanted.

'Why do you ask me if I wouldn't love to go into the desert, when you know as well as I do I wouldn't. We've talked about it over and over. Every few days we talk about it.' Although the sun was beating down on her chest, making it feel on fire, deep inside she could still feel the cold current that seemed to run near her heart.

'Well,' he said. 'You change. Sometimes you say you *would* like to go.'

It was true. She did change. Sometimes she would run to him with bright eyes. 'Let's go,' she would say. 'Let's go into the desert.' But she never did this if she was sober.

There was something wistful in his voice, and she had to remind herself that she wanted to feel cranky rather than heartbroken. In order to go on talking she said: 'Sometimes I feel like going, but it's always when I've had something to drink. When I've had nothing to drink I'm afraid.' She turned to face him, and he saw that she was beginning to have her hunted expression.

'Do you think I *ought* to go?' she asked him.

'Go where?'

'To the desert. To live in an oasis.' She was pronouncing her words slowly. 'Maybe that's what I should do, since I'm your wife.'

'You must do what you really want to do, he said. He had been trying to teach her this for twelve years.

'What I really want. . . . Well, if you'd be happy in an oasis, maybe I'd really want to do that.' She spoke hesitantly, and there was a note of doubt in her voice.

'What?' He shook his head as if he had run into a spiderweb. 'What is it?'

'I meant that maybe if you were happy in an oasis I would be, too. Wives get pleasure out of making their husbands happy. They really do, quite aside from its being moral.'

He did not smile. He was in too bad a humor. 'You'd go to an oasis because you wanted to escape from Western civilization.'

'My friends and I don't feel there's any *way* of escaping it. It's not interesting to sit around talking about industrialization.'

'What friends?' He liked her to feel isolated.

'Our friends.' Most of them she had not seen in many years. She turned to him with a certain violence. 'I think you come to these countries so you can complain. I'm tired of hearing the word *civilization*. It has no meaning. Or I've forgotten what it meant, anyway.'

The moment when they might have felt tenderness had passed, and secretly they both rejoiced. Since he did not answer her, she went on. 'I think it's uninteresting. To sit and watch costumes disappear, one by one. It's uninteresting even to mention it.'

'They are not costumes,' he said distinctly. 'They're simply the clothes people wear.'

She was as bitter as he about the changes, but she felt it would be indelicate for them both to reflect the same sorrow. It would happen some day, surely. A serious grief would silence their argument. They would share it and not be able to look into each other's eyes. But as long as she could she would hold off that moment.

LILA and FRANK

Frank pulled hard on the front door and opened it with a jerk, so that the pane of glass shook in its frame. It was his sister's custom never to go to the door and open it for him. She had an instinctive respect for his secretive nature.

He hung his coat on a hook in the hall and walked into the parlor, where he was certain he would find his sister. She was seated as usual in her armchair. Next to her was a heavy round table of an awkward height which made it useful for neither eating nor writing, although it was large enough for either purpose. Even in the morning Lila always wore a silk dress, stockings, and well-shined shoes. In fact, at all times of the day she was fully dressed to go into the town, although she seldom ventured from the house. Her hair was not very neat, but she took the trouble to rouge her lips.

'How were the men at the Coffee Pot tonight?' she asked when her brother entered the room. There was no variety in the inflection of her voice. It was apparent that, like him, she had never tried, either by emphasis or coloring of tone, to influence or charm a listener.

Frank sat down and rested for a while without speaking.

'How were the men at the Coffee Pot?' she said again with no change of expression.

'The same as they always are.'

'You mean by that, hungry and noisy.' For an outsider it would have been hard to say whether she was being critical of the men at the Coffee Pot or sincerely asking for information. This was a question she had asked him many times, and he had various ways of answering, depending upon his mood. On this particular night he was uncommunicative. 'They go to the Coffee Pot for a bite to eat,' he said.

She looked at him. The depths of her dark eyes held neither warmth nor comfort. 'Was it crowded?' she asked.

He considered this for a moment while she watched him attentively. He was near the lamp and his face was raspberry-colored, an even deeper red than it would have been otherwise.

'It was.'

'Then it must have been noisy.' The dropping of her voice at the end of a sentence gave her listener, if he was a stranger, the impression that she did not intend to continue with the conversation. Her brother of course knew this was not the case, and he was not surprised at all when a minute later she went on. 'Did you speak with anyone?'

'No, didn't.' He jumped up from his chair and went over to a glass bookcase in the corner. 'I don't usually, do I?'

'That doesn't mean that you won't does it?' she said calmly.

'I wouldn't change my habits from one night to the next,' he said. 'Not sitting at the Coffee Pot.'

'Why not?'

'It's not human nature to do that, is it?'

'I know nothing about human nature at all,' she said. 'Nor do you, for that matter. I don't know why you'd refer to it. I do suspect, though, that I at least might change very suddenly.' Her voice remained indifferent, as though the subject were not one which was close to her. 'It's a feeling that's always present with me . . . here.' She touched her breast.

Although he wandered around the room for a moment feigning to have lost interest in the conversation, she knew this was not so. Since they lied to each other in different ways, the excitement they felt in conversing together was very great.

'Tell me,' she said. 'If you don't expect to experience anything new at the Coffee Pot, why do you continue to go there?' This too she had often asked him in the past weeks, but the repetition of things added to rather than detracting from the excitement.

'I don't like to talk to anybody. But I like to go out,' he said. 'I may not like other men, but I like the world.'

'I should think you'd go and hike in the woods, instead of sitting at the Coffee Pot. Men who don't like other men usually take to nature, I've heard.'

'I'm not interested in nature, beyond the ordinary amount.'

They settled into silence for a while. Then she began to question him again. 'Don't you feel uneasy, knowing that most likely you're the only man at the Coffee Pot who feels so estranged from his fellows?'

He seated himself near the window and half

smiled. 'No,' he said. 'I think I like it.'

'Why do you like it?'

'Because I'm aware of the estrangement, as you call it, and they aren't.' This too he had answered many times before. But such was the faith they had in the depth of the mood they created between them that there were no dead sentences, no matter how often repeated.

'We don't feel the same about secrets,' she told him. 'I don't consider a secret such a great pleasure. In fact, I should hesitate to name what my pleasure is. I simply know that I don't feel the lack of it.'

'Good night,' said Frank. He wanted to be by himself. Since he very seldom talked for more than ten or fifteen minutes at a time, she was not at all surprised.

She herself was far too excited for sleep at that moment. The excitement that stirred in her breast was familiar, and could be likened to what a traveler feels on the eve of his departure. All her life she had enjoyed it or suffered from it, for it was a sensation that lay between suffering and enjoyment, and it had a direct connection with her brother's lies. For the past weeks they had concerned the Coffee Pot, but this was of little importance, since he lied to her consistently and had done so since early childhood. Her excitement had its roots in the simultaneous rejection and acceptance of these lies, a state which might be compared to that of the dreamer when he is near to waking, and who knows then that he is moving in a dream country which at any second will vanish forever, and yet is unable to recall the existence of his own room. So Lila moved about in the vivid world of her brother's lies, with the full awareness always that just beyond them lay the amorphous and hidden world of reality. These lies which thrilled her heart seemed to cull their exciting quality from her never-failing consciousness of the true events they concealed. She had not changed at all since childhood, when to expose a statement of her brother's as a lie was as unthinkable to her as the denial of God's existence is to most children. This treatment of her brother, unbalanced though it was, contained within it both dignity and merit, and these were reflected faithfully in her voice and manner.

FRIDAY

He sat at a little table in the Green Mountain Luncheonette apathetically studying the menu. Faithful to the established tradition of his rich New England family, he habitually chose the cheapest dish listed on the menu whenever it was not something he definitely abhorred. Today was Friday, and there were two cheap dishes listed, both of which he hated. One was haddock and the other fried New England smelts. The cheaper meat dishes had been omitted. Finally, with compressed lips, he decided on a steak. The waitress was barely able to hear his order.

'Did you say steak?' she asked him.

'Yes. There isn't anything else. Who eats haddock?'

'Nine tenths of the population.' She spoke without venom. 'Look at Agnes.' She pointed to the table next to his.

Andrew looked up. He had noticed the girl before. She had a long freckled face with large, rather roughly sketched features. Her hair, almost the color of her skin, hung down to her shoulders. It was evident that her mustard-colored wool dress was homemade. It was decorated at the throat with a number of dark brown woollen balls. Over the dress she wore a man's lumber jacket. She was a large-boned girl. The lower half of her face was long and solid and insensitive-looking, but her eyes, Andrew noted, were luminous and starry.

Although it was bitterly cold outside, the lunch room was steaming hot and the front window had clouded over.

'Don't you like fish?' the girl said.

He shook his head. Out of the corner of his eye he had noticed that she was not eating her haddock. However, he had quickly looked away, in order not to be drawn into a conversation. The arrival of his steak obliged him to look up, and their eyes met. She was gazing at him with a rapt expression. It made him feel uncomfortable.

'My name is Agnes Leather,' she said in a hushed voice, as if she were sharing a delightful secret. 'I've seen you eating in here before.'

He realized that there was no polite way of remaining silent, and so he said in an expressionless voice, 'I ate here yesterday and the day before yesterday.'

'That's right.' She nodded. 'I saw you both times. At noon yesterday, and then the day before a little later than that. At night I don't come here. I have a family. I eat home with them like everybody else in a small town.' Her smile was warm and intimate, as if she would like to include him in her good fortune.

He did not know what to say to this, and asked himself idly if she was going to eat her haddock.

'You're wondering why I don't touch my fish?' she said, catching his eye.

'You haven't eaten much of it, have you?' He coughed discreetly and cut into his little steak, hoping that she would soon occupy herself with her meal.

'I almost never feel like eating,' she said. 'Even though I do live in a small town.'

'That's too bad.'

'Do you think it's too bad?'

She fixed her luminous eyes upon him intently, as if his face held the true meaning of his words, which might only have seemed banal.

He looked at the long horselike lower half of her face, and decided that she was unsubtle and strong-minded despite her crazy eyes. It occurred to him that women were getting entirely too big and bony. 'Do I think what's too bad?' he asked her.

'That I don't care about eating.'

'Well, yes,' he said with a certain irritation. 'It's always better to have an appetite. At least, that's what I thought.'

She did not answer this, but looked pensive, as if she were considering seriously whether or not to agree with him. Then she shook her head from side to side, indicating that the problem was insoluble.

'You'd understand if I could give you the whole picture,' she said. 'This is just a glimpse. But I can't give you the whole picture in a lunchroom. I know it's a good thing to eat. I know.' And as if to prove this, she fell upon her haddock and finished it off with three stabs of her fork. It was a very small portion. But the serious look in her eye remained.

'I'm sorry if I startled you,' she said gently, wetting her lips. 'I try not to do that. You can blame it on my being from a small town if you want, but it has nothing to do with that. It really hasn't. But it's just impossible for me to explain it all to you, so I might as well say I'm from a small town as to say my name is Agnes Leather.'

She began an odd nervous motion of pulling at her wrist, and to his surprise shouted for some hotcakes with maple syrup.

At that moment a waitress opened the door leading into the street, and put down a cast-iron cat to hold it back. The wind blew through the restaurant and the diners set up a clamor.

'Orders from the boss!' the waitress screamed. 'Just hold your horses. We're clearing the air.' This airing occurred every day, and the shrieks of the customers were only in jest. As soon as the clouded glass shone clear, so that the words GREEN MOUNTAIN LUNCHEONETTE in reverse were once again visible, the waitress removed the iron cat and shut the door.

ARENA

FOR FURTHER INFORMATION
ABOUT ARENA BOOKS,
PLEASE WRITE TO
Arena Books
17 Conway Street
London W1P 6JD

ARENA